Evan in the Afterlife

JAMES BURROW

2

3

CONTENTS

A Timely Death   Pg 6

St Peter   Pg 8

Boarding Purgatory   Pg 13

Interdimensional Jellyfish   Pg 22

Sailing past the Shores of Hell   Pg 33

Trip to Mount Purgatory   Pg 37

The Void   Pg 47

The Lonely Jellyfish Herder   Pg 54

The Purging Deck   Pg 60

The Captain's Dinner Party   Pg 66

Heaven Dawns   Pg 87

Working and Wondering in Paradise   Pg 91

Immortally Binding Contract   Pg 103

Getting into Hell   Pg 106

Information Retrieval   Pg 109

The Brotherhood of Soul Releasers   Pg 114

Satan's Personal Assistant   Pg 123

5

The Secret Vegetable Garden   Pg 129

Circle of Evil   Pg 132

The Purgatory Plan   Pg 137

Scaling Mount Purgatory   Pg 143

Second Coming Ward   Pg 149

Heaven Prepares for Battle   Pg 158

Utopia   Pg 172

A Timely Death

Evan got up. It was the kind of getting out of bed that most working people would frown upon; not to mention nature's early risers who potter away the morning hours, reading the paper and doing other quiet, solitary activities, until the rest of the household awakes. Evan did, in fact, wake at six o'clock, but only because his bedroom faced east. This meant that the most annoying early riser, the Sun, beamed ferociously through his flimsy curtains. He scrunched his eyes against the light, but the muscle activity brought him further out of sleep. The same as every summer's morning, he made a half-hearted mental note to invest in a blind, but knew at the same moment that his ability to remember mental notes was hampered by his messy mind. As he reached for the mobile phone on the ledge above his bed, he noted the time and put the phone back. He forgot the time which he had just noted and so looked again. Six-fifteen. There was a time in his life when he would have flirted with the idea of going for a brisk morning jog, but that was long ago; at the age of twenty-four, Evan considered himself past the age of thinking about such sprightly things. He punched his pillows back into shape, rolled over to a cooler part of the mattress and let the heavy drapes of sleep descend on him. This was his favourite part of the day, going back to sleep after first waking up: it is when he had his best dreams.

Whilst the rest of the country was getting up for work, Evan was on a bus sitting next to an aristocratic giraffe, that was daintily smoking a cigarette. Whilst the rest of the country was spreading marmalade on pieces of toast, Evan had arrived at the alien zoo and was helping to feed the aliens, whose digestive systems functioned only in bubbles. Whist the rest of the country...well you get the idea.

Evan emerged into consciousness at around eleven, still groggy, but decided to venture from his bed all the same. He stumbled like a scarecrow into the shower and began a typical day. Typical that is, apart from the fact that he was about to die.

Evan's death reflected his life: slothful, pathetic, with a pinch of cowardice. The cause of death was a biscuit, a small round ginger one. It was the last biscuit in the pack and in his grandparents' cupboard. He knew that his granddad liked them, and would have wanted one on his return from visiting Evan's grandmother in hospital. His inner demons, however, won through yet again, and he consumed it in greedy guilt. He ate the Ginger Nut with such speed, to destroy the evidence of his shameful actions, that he forgot to chew, and it lodged in his throat, like a bath plug. After a sojourn thrashing around on the kitchen linoleum, Evan realised that the end had come and let death take him.

His life flashed before his eyes.

He nearly missed it.

St Peter

Rising to his knees Evan panted and looked around. He was standing on a lush green hillock that rose to its peak a hundred metres in front of him. Upon the hillock there was a neoclassical gate; its marble columns were set firmly in place, supporting immense white orbs. Between the columns there was a white, inviting light. Dwarfed by this structure stood a man dressed in white robes. His long beard joined his robes as they danced in the breeze that swept over the Sun-drenched hillock. Evan walked toward the Pearly Gates. As he approached, the man broke from contemplation and outstretched his arms to Evan. The Gate, man and grass seemed to pulsate gently with every heartbeat.

'I am St Peter,' the man said, 'you have died, and now your life must be judged in the eyes of God.' He spoke in a matter-of-fact way, which broke from the spiritual ambience of the Pearly Gates, and his flowing robes. As Evan inspected further, he could see a collar and tie peeking out from under his robes. He was also wearing polished leather shoes.

'Do you wish to enter the eternal paradise of Heaven?' St Peter continued, half turned to the Pearly Gates, his outstretched arms clad in loose fabric that fluttered in the breeze, revealing a set of cuff links. 'Do you wish to live alongside The Almighty and all of the Heavenly Hosts as a pure soul? To be endlessly fulfilled with love and forever at peace?'

Evan nodded.

'Are you ready for your Final Judgement?'

Evan shook his head.

'Oh well, if you follow me to my office, we can commence,' St Peter said and then waddled slowly away from the gates; his shiny black shoes squeaked as he made his way over the other side of the grassy hillock, out of sight. Evan followed. Beyond the Pearly Gates was a yellow portacabin, on breeze blocks. Stumpy, rusted iron legs supported the cumbersome yellow box, that was St Peter's office. Tufts of long grass sprouted around the mounts, and algae stained the single pane viewing window. St Peter opened the chipboard door.

Despite the exterior, the office was clean and tidy. St Peter was now behind him, closing the door with some string. He motioned a friendly gesture for Evan to sit in front of a hardwood desk, opposite St Peter's own black leather chair. As he settled down, Evan noticed a man in the corner of the cabin, sitting at a small desk, poring over paperwork and chewing a pencil. More than chewing, the man was shredding it to bits.

'How are we coming along Ivan?' St Peter asked the man, who looked about sixty years of age. Ivan looked up with a pitiable expression.

'I still don't understand,' Ivan said quietly, 'It asks in section C, part four: "Why did you swing your cat Mouldy around by its legs when you were seven?"'

'Don't worry, the P666 can be difficult, just do what you can,' St Peter said sympathetically as he pulled off his beard; climbed out of his white robes and hung them up on a peg behind the door. Without the biblical clothing to conceal his heavy frame and charcoal suit, the last remnants of the ethereal holy man were swept away. He had the look of a bumbling bureaucrat. He ran a hand through his thinning hair, as he landed heavily on his swivel chair.

'Sorry about the holy man business; it gives the right impression to our traditionally minded clients...' St Peter started, and then noticed that Evan was looking at the steel executive toy on his desk.

'You can push it if you like; it's John the Baptist baptising Jesus of Nazareth. The crafts club made it,' he said with a hint of pride. 'Ha, look at John's big beard. He looks like a big bearded, big wild bearded thing! Go on, give it a push.'

Evan obliged. The mechanism kicked in and they sat in silence, watching Jesus bob up and down.

'Right then, down to business,' St Peter said whilst clicking on his mouse and turning his attention to the computer screen. 'This looks clean: no mortal sins, plenty of charity work, and a lot of goodwill to all men. Well done, Evan, you've lived a very good life.'

'Charity work?' Evan asked, unaware of any charity work he had done.

'Your modesty is admirable Mr Edwards. You talk as if you don't remember funding a Kenyan hospital, a Zambian school, and the drilling of many wells across the African continent.'

Ivan suddenly looked up from his P666 with a look of shock, 'That was me! I did all of that! There's been a mix up!!'

'Please Ivan. We do not make mistakes. The computer system is new and probably infallible,' St Peter rebuked.

'I need a second opinion Mr Peter!' Ivan growled.

'I'm afraid you'll find that Christ gave me, and only me, the keys to Heaven,' St Peter said.

'Sorry about that Mr Edwards,' he said to Evan.

'Mr Edwards! I'm Mr Edwards. Mr Ivan Edwards,' Ivan said.

'Yes, I know,' St Peter said, 'I know this can be a very stressful time, but if you could bear with us.'

Evan remembered mention of his former cat Mouldy, connected it with Ivan's outburst and realised what had happened. He had never been a cheater in life: being a loser entirely on his own merits. This, though, was his final judgement; if there was ever a time to tell a little white lie...

'Yes, that was me,' he said woodenly, forcing the words out.

'However, with the good news comes the bad,' St Peter continued.

'Bad news? But surely once I've passed, I've passed, playing the harp forever?' Evan said nervously.

A scowl to appear on St Peter's flabby face.

'Your situation is not a case of either Heaven or Hell. Rest assured, you will be going to the eternal paradise of Heaven, however, at the moment you are not pure enough to be in the company of the Almighty,' he said as he unsuccessfully tried to steeple his fingers.

'I thought that he, I mean, I, had led a good life?' Evan said trying to ignore his conscience, which was informing him that he was sending an innocent man to Hell.

'No one is perfect: it says on your file that you have enjoyed eating shelled creatures; The Book of Leviticus forbids this. You, like most of our successful applicants, must first be purged of your sins in Purgatory.'

'Purgawhat?'

St Peter sighed and shook his head.

'Purgatory is a dimension where people who have committed venial sins go to be purged by immense pains, before entry to Heaven. The number and severity of your sins determine the length of your stay on Purgatory, and the intensity of purging. Any questions?'

Evan thought back over the wave of theology that had cascaded over his head. It was all ridiculous to him, however, one part of St Peter's speech nagged in his mind.

'When you said, "*on* Purgatory", surely you meant *in* Purgatory?'

St Peter let out a slow smile.

'*On* Purgatory, as in, on the vessel which traverses the inter-dimensional ether to pick up sinners from Earth, and deliver pure souls to the shores of Heaven. Finished Ivan?' he said turning to the man in the corner. Ivan nodded morosely.

'Good, just bring over your form and I shall take you to your eternal suffering.'

Ivan rose and shuffled across the portacabin to hand over his P666. St Peter scanned it with a practised eye. He filed the form; then rose to see Ivan out of his office, with a sympathetic hand on his shoulder.

'I don't understand,' Ivan sobbed, 'I can't remember doing any of the things you say are on my file. I don't remember swinging my cat around by its legs. I didn't have a cat called Mouldy: I'm allergic to cats.'

'The mind has a way of suppressing things we'd rather not remember,' St Peter soothed.

'Could you check again, just in case there's been a mistake?' Ivan pleaded.

'I don't see the point. Like I said, our computer system is probably infallible.'

St Peter came back into the cabin and exhaled heavily.

'Never gets any easier,' he sighed as he slumped back into his chair. With a grin on his face, he leaned forward and pushed the executive toy. 'John the Baptist with a big bushy beard, ha! Who'd have thought it eh?! Come on then, follow me.'

Boarding Purgatory

Purgatory glided toward the jetty. Black smoke billowed out of its rear funnel. She slowed on the approach, let out a couple of deafening blasts, then slid perfectly abreast. A causeway was lowered. Crew members emerged and began to set something up on the jetty. Once complete, A blond, fresh faced man bounded up to the confused group and beckoned them with enthusiasm to follow him and line up, ready for their 'snap-shots'. The weary and dishevelled, newly deceased passengers, were ushered to the stool; the photographer would ask them to sit up straight and "smile like a sinner."

Evan was shown to his cabin. Pieces of artwork lined the walls, hung in the spaces between the rows of cabin doors - replicas of famous Christian art throughout the ages. A couple of paintings caught his eye: The first was of a Seventeenth Century galleon complete with three sturdy masts and billowing sails, the weathered lettering of "Purgatory" was just visible on its tarred, oak hull, at the bottom was the inscription "1678 – 1730"; the second painting was of a large steam ship, its grey metal hull displaying the same word - "Purgatory" and below was the inscription "1862 – 1916". Once inside the cabin, he glanced around and saw an envelope on his bed, which he opened. Inside was a letter, which read:

Dear Mr Edwards,

I have, today, received notification of your misplacement. A computing error, very much in your favour, has placed you with us on Purgatory instead of Hell, where a Mr Ivan Edwards now undeservedly resides. Unfortunately, there is no recourse available to Ivan, as Hell is outside our influence. I have had a lengthy discussion with St Peter about the matter, and he feels that sending you to Hell as well would upset the balance of his accounts. He did, however, feel that placing you under an immortally binding contract with Heaven, would be appropriate. You will therefore be at the behest of the Heavenly Host, rather than purely a resident there; subject to any request made of you by either the angels or the council. This contract will also be in lieu of your purging. Any significant misbehaviour on your part, will result in the termination of the contract and your removal to Hell. I will assume in advance, unless I hear otherwise, that you agree to all terms and conditions.

Yours Sincerely,

Maggie Richards,
Purging Supervisor.

Evan placed the letter on the bed and decided that he needed a drink. He got up and made his way to the narrow corridor. He came out onto the wide, elegant stairwell, which he had passed through on his way to his cabin. It had deep red carpet and highly polished chrome hand railings. Evan found a diagram of the ship bolted to the wall. The main stairwell was the thoroughfare of the ship, connecting all ten levels. The nearest place to get a drink was known as the Mezzanine Bar on the sixth deck. He made his way sheepishly up the stairs.

The Mezzanine Bar was a large open plan room, with a long bar on the left and seating to the right. The walls were a deep purple and there were French windows to the rear, leading out to open air decking.

He went over to the barman and asked for a cider. A heavily built man in worn looking clothing was sat further along the bar, but did not acknowledge Evan's presence, or the existence of anything around him. His world seemed to have shrunk to the drink in front of him, which he cradled in a protective manner, as if invisible forces were about to snatch it from his grasp.

Evan sat at a table and sipped his cider. It was only moments before a lean man, in a cream linen suit, sidled up to his table.

'Mind if I sit here?' the man said but did not wait for a response, leaping into the seat opposite Evan.

'Gerard's the name and remittance is my game,' the man said shaking Evan's hand and pulling a business card from his inside pocket.

'Can I ask you? Are you a sinner? Yes,' Gerard said before Evan could say anything, 'otherwise you wouldn't be here, right?' Evan didn't try to react, he sensed that Gerard's questions would be answered by Gerard.

'You're a sinner and now you have to pay the price. You have to be purged by agony, until your debt to God is cleared,' he stated, before leaning in and speaking more quietly. 'At least that's what the powers-that-be say.' His eyes began to dart. 'There is another way. My business offers a unique service to people like yourself. Under the radar, if you understand my meaning. Imagine for a moment that your pain could be significantly reduced whilst on Purgatory. I have two hundred employees in Calcutta who will pray in shifts for you, so that your suffering can be reduced.'

The scruffy man, sat at the bar, spoke up, 'Until they finish their shift, go home, and pray to Vishnu!'

'Quiet Derek!' Gerard said before turning back to Evan. 'Don't listen to him, he's just a crazy person. All that I ask in return is the full value of your Will,' he said pulling a document from his satchel. 'All you have to do is sign this and I'll do the rest; how does that sound?'

'Exploitative!' the man at the bar heckled.

The French windows burst open, and an elderly man came running into the Mezzanine Bar; he was naked except for a nautical hat; his flaccid skin wobbled all over as he ran bare foot.

'Hideous! Pain like nothing you have ever known! Stay clear! Stay well clear from deck one! They will torture your very soul until it screams out for mercy but there is no mercy, not on this ship! No compassion, just brutality!' he shouted with a croaky voice.

Two crew members came running in after him. The naked man made a run for the stairwell, but they apprehended him; the nautical hat was removed, and his frail body cajoled into leaving.

'See what you could be avoiding,' Gerard said.

'Oh, give it up Gerard,' the scruffy man said, swivelling on his bar stool to face them, 'leave the boy alone; he probably doesn't have more than a worthless heap of a car to part with.'

Gerard looked at Evan.

'I don't even have that, actually,' Evan said.

'It was nice to have met you,' Gerard evacuated the table, in the time it takes to sneeze.

Evan got up and went over to the bar, 'Thanks for getting rid him,' Evan said standing next to the hunched figure. 'Can I get you a drink?'

'By all means boy. I'll have a quadruple whisky.'

Evan looked at the drinks list to see what this abuse of generosity was going to cost.

Evan and Derek propped up the Mezzanine bar on the sixth deck of Purgatory. Evan sipped at cider, whilst Derek gulped at whisky.

'Christianity is a strange thing,' Derek said. 'It reminds me of a story I heard about a missionary who was preaching the gospel and message of Jesus to an Inuit settlement. She spent many months telling them about Heaven and Hell and that if they did not turn to Jesus, they would certainly go to Hell. One day the chief Inuit took the missionary to one side and asked her: "if you had not told us about Jesus, would we have gone to Hell?" the missionary thought for a while and replied,
"No, I suppose not."
"Then why", asked the Inuit earnestly, "did you tell us?"'

'Is that true? That if you have never heard about Jesus then you don't go to Hell when you die?' Evan said.

'Some believe it to be true.'

'What happens to them then?'

'They probably go to the afterlife of whatever religion they were following before they died.'

'So, you think there are other afterlives? Other than the Christian one?'

'I'd say it is possible. It is a geographical tombola as to which religion you follow. In Europe and America, you have Christianity, but when you go east, to the Middle East, Islam dominates. And what about south into Africa where many countries are still dominated by diverse tribal religions. Then you get to the India and Hinduism. Then up to the Himalayas and Buddhism. Then down into China and Taoism. For most people, where you are born has a much stronger influence on your choice of religion than any independent thought or faith.'

There was a loud horn blast, and the bar began to vibrate.

'On to Heaven,' Derek said sardonically. Evan got up, slid back the French windows and stepped into the balmy air, as Purgatory slipped her moorings and chugged out. Evan stood beside the railings, enjoying the smell of the salty air and blue-green sea. There was a strange darkness to the horizon. As the ship went further, he saw that there was a membrane between the sea and the darkness beyond. Suddenly, the ship was passing though the shimmering membrane, the front of the vessel still visible as it sailed into the darkness. Evan gulped, gripped the railings and closed his eyes. When they opened, he was in twilight, with light coming from the other side of the membrane. Then the lights on deck came on and he could see only a short distance forward, but there was nothing there, just blackness. He went back to the Mezzanine Bar a little shaken. Derek greeted him with a knowing smirk.

'There's a first time for everything,' he said.

'What is it, out there?' Evan asked.

'That's the inter-dimensional ether. Sit down and tell me about yourself.'

'What's to tell?' Evan said. 'I wasn't up to much; thought I'd get going later in life, but then this happened.'

'There must have been something, someone?'

'There was Suzi...'

The bright halogen lights set into the wall were doing their best to illuminate the room. But the deep, thick darkness of the inter-dimensional ether oozed through the viewing windows. They continued to drink.

'How did you escape Hell?' Evan asked.

'A little presumptuous. Beneath my rough exterior there could be a heart of gold,' Derek replied.

Evan looked at him.

'I argued my case with St Peter,' Derek said.

'The bureaucrat? Surely he would be the last person to bend the rules for anyone.'

'I know. It was pure attrition followed by one good theological argument. In other words, I ground him down and then gave him one good reason to let me through and out of his face. I started with a barrage of philosophical arguments as to why I should not be sent to Hell. I began by arguing that if Plato's theory of the world of the "Forms" was correct, it meant that I sitting in St Peter's office was the perfect and everlasting Form of my previous Earthly self and by that logic it would be wrong for him to send me to Hell. Plato's made the point that, for example, on Earth there are millions of imperfect horses, with chipped hooves and worn teeth. But on a higher plane exists the eternal and Perfect Form of "a horse". And if you think about it, if Plato was right, then we are those Perfect Forms.'

'Perfect Forms?'

'Of our former Earthly selves. At least I know I am.'

Evan placed his glass on the bar and beheld Derek with his shabby beard containing alcohol moistened crumbs, his string vest complete with stains, frayed tweed jacket and hunched posture.

'Yes, I see your point,' Evan said, not quite knowing whether he was making fun or not.

'Then I moved onto Thomas Aquinas' argument that God gives everyone and everything a purpose, thereby making all my sinful actions a direct result of God's intention for my life path. Next was the argument that my entire experience on Earth was driven by a malevolent demon intent on deceiving me as put forward by Rene Descartes. All my sins were a direct result of the actions of the wicked deceptions of Descartes' Demon, leaving the real me free from any sin.'

'By now, St Peter's eyebrows were furrowed in confusion. Throughout this, there was a steady stream of newly deceased people building up outside his office, waiting for their judgement. I then dived into Pascal's wager. The wager suggests that a gambler should believe in a God because if you believe in a God, and there is a God, than you gain eternal bliss; if there is no God, than the outcome is neutral. A betting man would therefore always believe in God. I argued that I wagered against God deliberately in protest against the sin of gambling itself and should be rewarded for my martyrdom.'

'I was being quite expressive and accidentally knocked over his little executive toy - two men humping, but what was really upsetting him, was the administrative backlog waiting on the hillock outside his office. At which point I started babbling on about how I couldn't possibly go to Hell due to Zeno's paradox of motion. The main thrust being that in order to reach the porthole to Hell, I would first have to walk to the halfway point; but before I reached the halfway point, I would have to walk the first quarter and the first eighth and sixteenth and so on. In other words, I would have to walk an *infinite number* of *finite* distances, which is completely impossible, according to Zeno. It was at this point that I was ready to deliver my final argument; the good theological argument: the one that would let me slip the noose of Hell.'

Derek pulled up the sleeves of his jacket and made two puppets out of his hands.

'"Give me one good reason not to send you to Hell," St Peter demanded, playing right into my hands.'

'"Alright I do have a reason: it is the fact that God gives us permission to mess up, to fail. Jesus taught us this in his parable of the Prodigal Son. The parable is about God's love being like the love of the father in the story. A love that is unyielding and unconditional. When the Prodigal Son had lost everything, he gained a tiny notion of how great and unconditional his father's love for him was. I am like the Prodigal Son; I have pushed away God's love all my life. I, like the son had access to my passions but believed that my passions were unwanted. In the parable, the prodigal is fully reunited with the father even though he has abused and shunned his love. The elder brother in the parable shunned the father's love also. By trying to earn his inheritance through hard labour, he tried to take away his father's capacity to give him unconditional love: he diminished the love gift of the father. Doing anything became a duty and not a joy. This is a son who pushed himself on, despised his brother and secretly resented his father. You have let into Heaven, those who have behaved like the elder brother, people who have tried to earn salvation by good works, would that be true?"

"Yes, that would be true,"' The hand representing St Peter admitted.

Derek wrapped his hand around his drink.

'The phone on his desk rang, it was his wife. She asked him who he was judging at that moment. He told her that I was an immoral rotter who thought I'd got an argument to stay out of Hell. She wanted to hear it, and so made St Peter hand over the phone! I re-told the story and handed the phone back, and she told St Peter to let me through to Purgatory. He filled in the paperwork, and I ended up here. No question about who wears the trousers in that marriage.'

'So, you're going to Heaven, eventually?' Evan asked.

'No, I got through to Purgatory but am permitted no further. I am Purgatory's only permanent resident.'

Interdimensional Jellyfish

Later, Derek turned up at Evan's cabin knocking wildly. Evan woke up, ending a dream about Suzi with a woodpecker drilling a hole in his head. He tore back the bed clothes, turned on the light and opened the door.

'What?' Evan demanded.

Derek swayed. The ship was rocking in the ether and so Evan gave him the benefit of the doubt: thirty percent the ship, seventy percent him being drunk.

'I had an idea,' Derek said through a grinning face.

'Couldn't it have waited?'

'No. Stop being such a wet flannel. It has to be rough on deck, or we'll get caught.'

This didn't sound good: "caught" meant doing something he shouldn't be doing. Doing something he shouldn't be doing meant breaking his immortally binding contract and a cast-iron, one-way ticket to the fires of Hell.

'No way Derek. If I put a foot wrong, you know I'm for it.'

'I know; but I also know that there is a certain young lady back on Earth who you might want to have a talk with, about Hell and Heaven being real?'

'Yes, but that's impossible now.'

'What if I told you that there is a way?'

Evan stood in his underwear thinking hard, gripping the cabin door to steady himself against the tumultuous movements of the ship. On the one hand he would be putting his own soul at great risk. But on the other hand, he had a chance to warn someone he loved that the afterlife was real, the only person who really meant anything to him.

'O.K then, give me a moment,' he said.

Derek explained how the ether was not always stable and that the boundaries of different dimensions clashed against each other. This caused friction to build up which was eventually released as large waves of energy, causing Purgatory to roll and yaw. Evan felt oddly buoyant as they made their way to the stern of the ship. He was on an adventure with real things at stake, a position that he had never experienced in his safe life on Earth. He was also still a little drunk from the cider.

Derek continued to explain that the rain falling on them in torrents was not rain at all, but fragments of good and evil fused together to produce a neutral liquid; fragments originating from Heaven and Hell. When they reached the stern of the ship, Derek signalled for them to stop. He took a quick glance over the railings, and then turned to give Evan a loaf of bread.

'What's this for?' he whispered.

'Wait a minute,' Derek whispered back, and began to take off his tired, brown tweed jacket, 'hold this as well,' he said flapping the jacket at Evan.

'Come on now, what are we doing?!' Evan hissed. The stress in his voice brought on by feeling like a wet pantry-come-coat stand.

'Here we are now,' Derek exclaimed as he began to pull something rope like from his abdominal area, 'hold the end of this. Now pull it as I spin around, and it should come free.'

He pulled and pulled whilst Derek span and span. Eventually they were both standing catching their breath, with about thirty foot of rope lying on the deck between them.

'Where on earth did you get that from?' Evan asked.

'What's wrong with it, perfectly good, properly tailored and everything. Well not tailored to *me* as such but still - a classic.'

'What? You had that length of rope tailored to you?'

'Oh, right, the rope, sorry, I thought you were making fun of my jacket.'

'Well, the jacket could probably do with a wash. I mean what's that?' Evan said pointing to one of the various stains which were so blatant that they could be seen in the poor lighting conditions.

'Give me that,' Derek snapped, snatching back his jacket, 'It doesn't need a wash, and anyway, everyone knows that good quality tweed washes itself. It's like hair; if you don't wash your hair for long enough, eventually it begins to clean itself. I mean look at hippies, they have dreadlocks, and they get more free love than a gigolo. No one wants to get romantic with anyone with smelly hair, do they? So, if it's true for hair, and my jacket is made of tweed, which is sort of a hair. I think it stands to reason that my jacket will wash itself.'

Derek dusted off the sleeves of his smelly jacket and stood tall, as a man who had successfully fought and won his argument.

'Right, and wearing that particular jacket, when was the last time you had a significant encounter with a woman?'

Derek ignored the gibe, maintaining a regal posture to show that such a petty witticism was beneath him.

'O.K let's get on with this before someone sees us,' Derek said levelly.

'Good idea. Can you tell me what we're doing? I mean you obviously enjoy keeping me in the dark...'

'You are going to lower me over the back of the ship using this rope so that I can collect something in my bucket.'

'Something?'

'And ruin the suspense? I'll tell you how I made the rope – to ease your curiosity. This rope is made from beer mats...Don't look at me like that, like I've gone stark raving mad. Not the cardboard ones, but the heavy duty, material ones used for wiping up spillages: everyone turns a blind eye to an alcoholic with a beer mat fetish.'

'Must have taken you a long time,' Evan said dryly

'Ten years give or take, but the rewards are obvious.'

They tied one end of the rudimentary, plated beer mat twine to the sturdy railing. Derek mounted the railings and lowered himself down on the outside of the hull. The mats stretched and made noises of protest. They were, after all, designed for a sedentary life on bar tops; they were not designed for daring escapades, involving holding the weight of an eighteen stone man.

Despite the protests, and to Evan's amazement, it held. He waited impatiently on the deck, darting his head and eyes from place to place, increasingly worried about the possibility of crew appearing from further up the ship. Evan looked out over the side and down into the murky darkness. He saw a body shaped blob, laboriously heaving itself up the rope, muttering to itself.

'Derek?'

'Ta-ke the buck-et will you?' he said with difficulty due to bucket handle being trapped in his mouth. Evan reached down and took it from him.

'Any crew about?' Derek asked quietly.

'Not now, but one came over earlier,' Evan jested.

'Really? How did you get rid of him?' Derek said amazed.

'I bribed him with the loaf of bread of course,' Evan said, failing to hold back laughter.

'Idiot,' Derek muttered. Evan grabbed his arms and heaved him back over the railings and safely onto the ship's deck.

'What was the bread actually for?' Evan asked.

'A cover story: if someone came past you could have told them you were feeding the jellyfish; some violent twitching would have to accompany that story, but my resources were limited.'

'Right, you realise that you are insane. Anyway, what *is* in there?'

'God knows,' Derek said, 'the remnants of a brain: a life's worth of self-taught philosophy tainted by traumatic experiences, marinated in some of the world's finest whiskies.'

Evan looked across at him in the darkness.
'Oh, in there!' Derek said pointing into the bucket. 'Those are inter-dimensional jellyfish my boy.'

They got back to Derek's cabin and shook their heads like shaggy dogs. Spraying the worst of the moisture over the fake mahogany walls. Derek slopped the jellyfish into the hand basin of his ensuite. Evan was transfixed by its alien appearance. Now out of the ether, the flesh was folded over itself like an origami project trodden on. The long strands of translucent tentacles spilled out over the basin. He plucked up the courage to lightly prod it with Derek's toothbrush.

It spasmed.

'Arh!' he squealed, 'It's still alive!'

'Course it's still alive,' came the muffled response from the next room. Derek finished wiping his face with a towel and joined him in the bathroom. 'It lives off energy waves. The light from the bathroom and your girlish screaming.'

'What are we going to do with it?'

'You are going to lie down on the bed and place it on your face, letting its tentacles worm into your ear holes, so that it can feed off your brainwaves.'

'Not a chance! I'm not putting that thing anywhere near me!'

'Oh come, come it's not as bad as it sounds. Tickles a bit as they go in but once attached the sensation is one of tranquillity.

Look you've done the hard part: we didn't get caught. So do you want to speak to what's-her-name or not?'

'Suzi. Yes of course. But how does it work? I mean what does the jellyfish do?'

'It transports your mind into the body of another person; you take over their body. Everyone on Earth and in the afterlife, has a counterpart jellyfish that is unique to them. Very few people know about this.'

'But how do you choose the right person? The jellyfish in your basin could belong to a child in Mozambique.'

'Every jellyfish has unique markings on its fleshy back: spots, stripes, concentric rings that identify it down to a specific person.'

'You can read the markings?'

'Not all of them. I know the markings for different countries and cities, but the ones that describe a specific person are harder to decipher. I spotted one from the Sultbury area floating past and so grabbed it. The rest is luck.'

Evan went into the ensuite and stood watching the squiggly jellyfish writhe in the hand basin. He picked it up at arm's length. It felt cold and wet. Lying down on Derek's bed, he slowly placed it on his face.

Yuk. The tentacles tickled around his earholes, before sliding in. Darkness enveloped him.

Evan opened his eyes: there was darkness. He fumbled around for a light switch and found it; magnolia walls surrounded him as he lay on an uncomfortable bed. He ripped back the bed clothes and beheld his emaciated, varicose veined legs. Getting up was a difficulty: his legs felt like lead as he swung them over onto the worn carpet. Pushing himself upright, he made it halfway before his right knee gave way, causing him to collapse to the ground with a thud and a wail of pain. After a few seconds a nurse came bustling in.

'What's wrong Mr Getty?' she said in a slow Jamaican accent.

'My knee!' Evan gasped in between jolts of pain.

'You silly man, you know that you can't put any weight on that knee.'

'No, I didn't!' Evan protested. The nurse sighed and helped him onto the bed.

'What are you doing up so late?'

'Inter-dimensional jellyfish catching. Where am I?' Evan asked.

'You're in your room Mr Getty.'

'I know that. Where am I in the country?'

'Sultbury,' she replied.

The nurse gave him a suffering look. This old body was going to cause him difficulties. He didn't know of its intricate limitations and needs like its real owner did, through a lifetime of getting old with it. He put most of his weight on his left knee and hobbled over to the mirror. Wispy grey hair combed over a bald head, sunken eyes with deep crow's feet on either side, untidy stubble, and loose skin hanging under his chin. Evan looked down at Mr Getty's watch - 01:03.

'I'd better be on my way. Which way is out?'

'You can't go out now, it's far too late, you might have a fall.'

'I don't care about that, I've got a soul to save,' he said as he rummaged in the wardrobe for something suitable to wear. All he could find was a large Macintosh overcoat. He wormed his bare, bony arms into the arm holes and then loosely tied it at the waist. He hobbled ungracefully out of the retirement home and caught the night bus into the centre of his old university town.

He hobbled down the steps of the bus and tried to get onto the pavement below. The gap between the bus and the pavement was something of an impassable void for this frail body. Evan clung to the bright yellow hand holds of the bus, extended his left leg (the one with the good knee) and made a leap of faith. God was apparently not with him or had gone to make a cup of tea, because Evan ended up face down on the pavement with blood spurting from a broken nose. A middle-aged woman helped him up. Evan said he was fine and accepted some tissue from her. He stuffed the tissue up both his nostrils, and then looked around at the familiar sight of his university town centre. It was half-one in the morning and the sound of loud dance music was seeping out of the night clubs. Groups of drunk students meandered their way along the High Street, barely giving him any notice. Apart from one man who asked him if he was going to flash for them. His best bet was a pub called the Indigo Flamingo, which was situated on a side street sandwiched between a bong shop and a tattoo parlour. This was where Suzi always used to hang out. Hopefully she still did.

The bouncer on the door looked at him from head to toe. Literally toe because he had forgotten to put on any shoes or socks during his brisk exit from the retirement home. His feet were black from the grime of the town pavements and his Mackintosh flapped loosely in the wind, just enough for the bouncer to see his pants beneath.

'Are you O.K mate?' the bouncer asked.

'I'm looking for someone,' Evan replied.

'I can't let you in looking like that,' the bouncer said. Evan felt a shifting in the lower half of Mr Getty's old body.

'I *need* to go in. *Please*. If you don't want a senior citizen soiling himself outside your establishment than I suggest that you let me in to use your facilities.'

'Alright than gramps, be quick.'

Evan walked in and started to scan the bar for Suzi. Looking back, he could see that the bouncer was busy talking to some students who had turned up too drunk to be worthwhile patrons of the Indigo Flamingo. So instead of heading for the toilets, he broke left and headed for the smoking garden: Suzi's favourite place due to her addiction to "Old Horn Blower" rolling cigarettes. She couldn't possibly smoke one of the main-stream brands of tobacco; she had to pick an obscure, extremely strong, only smoked by knurled old men, brand tobacco, just to be different. He had always joked with her that if there ever was a brand of tobacco called "Salty sea dog's alternative ship mate cure for North Atlantic induced rheumatism" She would switch.

He hobbled between the tall garden heaters. There were benches either side, but he already knew exactly where to look: the bench in the bottom left-hand side - her favourite spot. She could observe everyone coming in or going out, like a wannabe secret agent; the only career she would consider, if she weren't too busy being a "parasite of decent society". Then he saw her: black and purple hair falling loosely around her pale white face with big blue eyes, cigarette held luxuriantly in her hand. Evan stopped in his tracks, overcome with strong familiar feelings. Mr Getty's frail heart nearly exploded in his chest.

What was he supposed to do now? and who was that huge guy with the beard and tattoos sitting next to her? Evan kicked himself for the feelings of jealousy that washed over him. No matter how many new boyfriends Suzi had, Evan always felt the same stupid, futile, petty jealousy toward each and every one of them.

He decided to just walk up to them.

'Anyone sitting here?' he asked them whilst pointing to a space on the bench.

'Help yourself,' Suzi said chirpily; never one to judge on appearances, even a dribbling old man in a flasher's Mack. Then he clammed up: what on earth was he supposed to say? He remembered that she was into studies of the occult: mediums, electronic voice phenomenon. She might listen after all.

'I'm your dead friend Evan inhabiting a stranger's body,' he finally said.

There was a pause. Then Suzi's boyfriend told him to go away.

'I take it you mean Evan Edwards?' she asked genuinely intrigued.

'Yes.'

'What's Hell like Evan?' she said with a snigger.

'Don't joke, I nearly ended up there. I got out because of maladministration. That's what I wanted to talk to you about. Hell is real Suzi, and if you don't start making some changes, you're going to end up there.'

'You sound like my mum, you don't know me from Adam, and I'm bored with your little game of spin out the drunk chic. Just because you've watched all the repeats of Last of the Summer Wine and got a bit bored in your hovel of a sheltered accommodation basement flat, it doesn't give you the right to mess with people's heads.'

Her boyfriend stood up and moved over toward him.

'I can prove that I'm Evan! Just think of something that only we knew. I don't know, a shared joke or something!'

The boyfriend lifted Evan to his feet.

'O.K weirdo,' she said picking up her packet of "Old Horn Blower",' if I wasn't smoking this brand of tobacco, which would I smoke?'

Evan thought and smiled. He knew the answer to this one.

'Salty sea dog's alternative ship mate cure for North Atlantic induced rheumatism.'

Suzi let out a small gasp, 'Evan?!'

The boyfriend threw him to the floor. 'Stop messing with her head you...'

Evan didn't hear the rest of what he said because he woke up in Derek's cabin with a jellyfish suckered to his face. He pulled the slimy creature off, sat bolt upright, and gasped for air. He ran to the ensuite and vomited.

'Any success?' Derek enquired casually from the cabin.

'Yes, I think so.'

'Good.'

'Thanks Derek, I really owe you one.'

'Think nothing of it my boy.'

Evan wiped his mouth and walked back into the cabin to find Derek putting Mr Getty's counterpart Jellyfish into an old pickling jar.

'Derek?'

'Yes?' he said as he opened a bottom draw.

'How did you find out that putting a jellyfish on your face and letting it worm into your brain let you inhabit other people's bodies on Earth and in the afterlife?' he asked cagily.

Derek shrugged as he added the jar to the rest of his collection already in the draw, making a clinking noise.

'The same way that some bloke found out that you could milk a cow. Never be afraid to experiment with the unusual.'

Evan went back to his own cabin feeling that he had finally done something of significance with his life. It was a good feeling.

Sailing past the Shores of Hell

The crackle of the ships speaker system woke Evan from his slumber.

'Good afternoon, ladies and gentlemen,' the brisk and officious voice announced, 'The captain would like to make you aware that we will shortly be sailing past the shores of Hell. He would like to invite you to the Sun Deck for an excellent view as we cruise past. Refreshments will be provided. Thank you.'

He got out of bed, threw on his clothes and headed to the Sun Deck. It seemed that many of the passengers had been gripped by the same morbid curiosity, as port side was already beginning to fill with people. He got a space at the railings and waited. He saw Hell's dimensional membrane shimmer as the ship traversed near to it. Beyond the membrane there was a beach, spotted with bonfires and flaming torches; then they heard the screams. Long drawn out, pitiful gurgling screams which crescendo and then ebb away, only to be replaced by the next. The beach consisted of coarse sand, with craggy grey rocks jutting up. Red demons walked about, carrying instruments of pain: spears, whips and tridents. Hundreds of gaunt and sickly-looking men and women crawled and stumbled between the rocks in tattered clothes, screaming out in panic whenever a demon came close.

This was enough for some of the passengers who thought that it was inhumane to witness the misery of fellow human beings from the comfort of a cruise ship deck. They weaved back through the crowds with pursed lips and worried eyes. Most, however were held in a trance, squinting their greedy eyes to glimpse the fate they had all managed to evade.

Once the ship was past the apocalyptic scene; the passengers began to tire of straining their necks to get a last glimpse of Hell and decided that the newly arrived spread of savouries and cake was a more attractive proposition.

A commotion brewed further along the port deck. The crowd around him began to murmur. An elderly man next to Evan straightened up and looked over the crowd.

'Looks like the Mormons are leaving us,' he said, then nudged Evan. 'Maybe the mini casino was too much for them? I suppose they think they'll find a nice area of salt flats in the ether to settle on.' This contrasted to the hysterical woman behind him who had heard that the lifeboats were being lowered and thought the situation could be helped by shouting that the ship was sinking and everyone was going to die. A ripple of Chinese whispers went through the crowd and A man to Evan's right looked confused as to what a "Moorhen" was and why it was trying to row to the shores of Hell?

A small wooden lifeboat was now floating away from the hull of Purgatory. The two oars were manned by men in dowdy black clothes and black cloth hats. Two Mormons were sat at the bow and stern of the lifeboat looking very pleased with their accomplishment. Purgatory's crew members were at the empty space where the lifeboat would have been, shouting to the quickly departing Brethren of the Latter Day Saints. The hysterical woman behind Evan was now demanding to know why emergency protocols had changed from women and children first to reclusive Christian denominations first?

'Why are the Mormons rowing to Hell?' he asked the elderly man.

'Would religious fanaticism be a disappointingly obvious answer?'

Evan shrugged, 'Why don't they just accept that they're dead and move on?'

'Wise words young man. Unfortunately, those four in the wooden tub believe that the damned can still be saved. They're rowing to Hell armed with only a handful of Gideon New Testaments and absolutely no idea about what unspeakable horrors await them. You have to respect that if nothing else.'

The Mormon on the bow was now stood up on the prow of the boat with outstretched arms clasping a Bible, raising it aloft. As the beach was just going out of view, the lifeboat landed, and the Mormons were dragged away by a group of demons.

Evan went for the last slice of Victoria sponge, but his hand was met by another hand, slender and female and on the same trajectory as his own.

'Oh,' he said as he looked up to find that the owner of the rival hand was a beautiful young girl that he had not seen before. 'Sorry...did you want it?' he blurted.

'I was planning to get a bit of food before the rest of these vultures finish it all,' the girl said.

'It seems like watching others in pain builds appetite, which is a bit wrong, but I guess that's humanity for you...' Evan realised that he was rambling. 'You have it. I'm not really hungry,' he said.

'Thanks.'

'What did you make of it?' Evan asked.

'What Hell? I feel sorry for most of them. Some were probably good people. Don't you think it's weird how there might be some people we knew down there...' she mused.

'And now we're watching them as background entertainment?' Evan finished.

'Exactly,' she said. 'So why do you think they do it? Make such a big deal about looking at Hell I mean?' she asked.

Evan shrugged, 'So that we won't complain about the freshness of the lunch salad or the state of the swimming pool changing rooms?'

She stared blankly at him.

'I think it's a stark reminder about where we could all have so easily ended up. It makes us more appreciative of each moment of our own afterlife,' she said. She gazed up at him and smiled, 'Like now.'

Evan blushed and went a furious shade of red. He was determined to not let embarrassment get the better of him, not now, not when he was dead. He took in a slow controlled breath and forced himself to talk.

'Yes. Just like now.'

'I'm Jennifer, what's your name?'

Trip to Mount Purgatory

The next day, an object loomed. A mysterious shape in the black inter-dimensional ether. It resembled a volcanic island, circular in shape and about a mile in diameter. With a single, bluish mountain forcing its way into the ether. Its flanks were made up of seven flat levels cut into the rock in a terrace fashion: an oddity of creation within the ether that surrounded it on all sides, above and below. It had a base of rock which jutted downwards and inward; a mirror shape of the mountain above it.

The speaker system came on waking Evan from a light slumber.

'A good morning, ladies and gentlemen, this is your captain speaking. We will shortly be alongside Mount Purgatory. If you wish to go ashore and enjoy the tour of the mountain with our activities team then please report to the Auditorium in one hour's time. Thank you and I hope you have an enjoyable day.'

Evan groaned and rolled over in his bed, clasping a pillow to his ears to keep the captain's nasal voice from rousing him to full consciousness. Just as he was drifting off again, his cabin phone rang. He clumsily fought back the covers and spilled his body in the general direction of the ringing sound. Eyes not quite in focus, he misjudged the lunge of his hand, and sent the receiver clattering to the floor.

'Hello?' he finally said, now in partial control of his physical surroundings.

'Good morning, it's Jennifer,' she said sweetly. 'Having trouble?'

Evan sat bolt upright, 'Hi.'

'Did you hear the announcement?' Jennifer asked.

'Sort of, but I was trying to sleep through it, what was it about?'

'We're stopping off at Mount Purgatory for the day!'

'Mount Purgatory? Sounds painful.'

'No, no they don't use it for purging any more, not since the 1700s, since ships large enough to do the job became more efficient. It just drifts around the ether, moving with the wind and tides. It's all in a pamphlet I picked up today. So, are you coming?' she asked.

Evan had planned to spend the rest of the morning in bed, but an opportunity had presented itself and he had enough sense to go with it.

'Sure, I'll see you in the Auditorium.'

The Auditorium was bustling with passengers by the time Evan turned up. He saw Jennifer at one of the tables chatting to an old couple. He admired the way that she seemed able to do this. It was something that he had found difficult throughout his life. He wound his way up to the table and touched her on the shoulder.

'Hi Evan,' she said with a smile. Evan smiled back before sitting down. She introduced her new friends; Evan raised a sheepish hand to greet the two strangers. One of the activities team got onto the stage and asked them to fill in their shore passes which were being handed around. They were also given a strip of acetate transfer paper with three backward "P"s.

The passengers were led out to the deck on the port side, where they were told to wait with their lifejackets. They stood staring at the mountain that was now right next to them and rising loftily out of sight above them, where it was lost in the gloom. One of the passengers saw something approaching them from Mount Purgatory; he pointed and alerted the rest. Everyone strained their eyes, trying to penetrate the deep black of the ether. It was a boat with something standing up inside. Almost like a person; someone gasped "an angel!".

The boat that the angel piloted could have carried a hundred people. The angel stood in the centre of the vessel that leapt lightly through the ether. Propelled by the angel's outstretched, motionless wings, with no sailors or oars. The angel was the real business: sufficiently glorious that mortal eyes should shrink from him. The tourist passengers pointed and smiled. Some even clapped.

The angel brought his vessel alongside the port deck of Purgatory with some practised flicks and angling of his wings. The passengers and activities team clambered on board like a procession of bright orange lemmings. The angel looked down at the group of tourists and sighed. The angel tried to strike up the traditional song that had been sung on the boat to Purgatory for centuries. Using his sword like a conductor's baton, he sang *'In exitu Israel de Aegypto....'* After a verse and chorus, the angel was still singing alone, none of the passengers knew the words or the tune. Not even the activities team had learnt the Latin ditty. The traditional song faded embarrassingly. The activity co-ordinator then stood and started to sing *'row, row, row your boat,'* which was taken up with gusto.

He deposited the tourists on the beach at the base of the mountain. The activities co-ordinator rallied the tourists and started up the beach, leaving the angel to tidy up the bright orange lifejackets the passengers had stripped off.

They came to the gate of Mount Purgatory. At first it seemed to be a simple fissure in the wall of the rock; but as they approached it became clear that it was, in fact, a gateway entrance, with three steps before it that shone blindingly in three colours. The first was white marble, polished to a mirror finish; the second was basalt, coloured darker than purple, with a rough finish and two cracks along its length and width forming the sign of the Cross; the third and last was flaming porphyry, brighter red than arterial blood. The gate itself was of solid banded iron. In this blinding light sat the angelic gate keeper, as glorious as the one that brought them to the shore of the mountain. He sat on a granite block, his feet on the third step, holding a drawn sword with light reflecting from it like a bright flame. He wore a dusty-earth coloured robe.

'I am the gatekeeper,' the angel bellowed in a theatrical voice. 'I guard the gate into Mount Purgatory proper and well,' he said with a flourish of his sword. 'I will only allow through those who are sufficiently devout and those who have a valid reason through.'

The activities co-ordinator produced a thin wad of paper tickets and handed them to the gatekeeper. He tucked his sword under one arm and fumbled around for his ticket hole-punch machine with a "please bear with me" expression on his face. Once found, he punched the tickets and handed them back, before gripping his sword once more and resuming his role.

'I have in my possession two keys, one of silver and one of gold; both are needed to open the gate when used in order. These were given to me by St Peter who advised me to err on the side of generosity when using them.'

The activities co-ordinator caught the gatekeeper's eye and gestured for him to stop his speech.

'Sorry to interrupt,' she said producing a thicker wad of paper, 'but the gatekeeper has to sign all of our shore passes before we can go in: St Peter is very insistent.'

'God bless St Peter,' mumbled the gatekeeper, as he fumbled his robes for a pen.

Once all the papers had been signed, the gatekeeper turned his attention back to his audience. 'And now if you could find the acetate "P" strips that you were given earlier...that's it Madam...now place them against your forehead and rub hard...that's it.'

The gatekeeper paused as the rest of the tourists rubbed the transfers onto their foreheads.

'When Mount Purgatory was functional, the sinners would have seven "P"s cut into their foreheads,' the angel continued. 'As they successfully negotiated the seven levels of the mountain, they would have them erased one by one until all of their sins had been purged. They would then be able to pass through the porthole at the mountain's peak and emerge into Eden where they could talk directly with God Almighty. These transfer strips just to give you a taste of what it would be like.'

'Why do we only have three if there are seven levels?' Jennifer asked.

'Because you are only permitted to visit the first three levels of the mountain,' the gatekeeper replied.

The gatekeeper turned and opened the gate with his keys. The iron doors parted with a shrill shriek and clanged shut behind the party. The way up was narrow and difficult, with irregular rocks on both sides. The rocks protruded out at random, making the upward path slow to travel. The activities co-ordinator led the way up the sheer sided gully. Eventually they emerged onto the first terrace. It was flat and about thirty meters wide, with rock rising behind it and falling away before. The rock of the first terrace stretched away to the left and right. The cliff face had no visible way up to the next terrace, but was of clear white marble, carved with wonderful life-like sculptures giving examples of humility: angels, the Ark of the Covenant on a cart drawn by oxen. On the terrace itself were three still dummies, bent over with large burdens on their backs. Their prosthetic faces staring down at the floor of the terrace. They looked in a poor state of repair, with tufts of stuffing bursting out of the stitch-work on their faces, and their clothes were tatty. One had a missing arm that was leant up against one of its companions.

The activities co-ordinator pulled out a script and began to read from it.

'This is the first terrace where the sin of pride is purged. Around this terrace slowly move those purging their sins, each weighed down and bent over by a heavy burden, praying as they go. On the pavement itself, placed where the penitents cannot help but see them, bent under their loads as they are, are carvings as wondrous as those on the marble cliff face, giving examples of the sin of pride,' she looked up from the script.

'Any questions?'

But nobody asked. They all sensed that their guide knew nothing about the mountain except for what she was reading out.

She led them along the first terrace and followed the path as it curved around the mountain. Upon the steps to the second terrace sat another angel, white winged and white robed. He was having a cigarette. On seeing the party, he spluttered and extinguished it on the ancient marble steps. The activities co-ordinator gave him a chastising look as the angel rose to his feet, kicking the butt away.

'Pray, may we progress to the second terrace, the terrace of the envious?' she asked the angel.

'Yes of course,' the angel said drawing to his full height, bringing his gleaming sword to bear in front of him, 'but first I must remove a "P" from each of the foreheads of these sinners.'

There was a worried pause.

'This is where you lick your finger and rub off a "P" from your forehead,' the angel explained.

Once done, they trudged up the flight of marble steps. At the top of the stairs, they came across another terrace like the first except that the rock and pavements were bare.

'This is the terrace of the envious,' said the activities co-ordinator. 'The penitents here sit, dressed in hair cloth, along the inner edge of the terrace. Their eyelids are sewn together with threads of iron, and they resemble blind beggars who constantly sigh. They warn passers-by of the dangers of envy.'

Even though they were dummies, the tourists all gasped when they saw the camouflaged figures up against the rock with their eyelids sewn shut. On cue a speaker embedded in the rock face crackled into life.

'Be warned brothers and sisters,' the speaker said, 'for you see that I have been envious and thus are being punished accordingly...um...so don't be envious.'

The co-ordinator looked ahead to the next flight of steps at another angel who had been roped into pandering to the human tourists. The angel gave the co-ordinator a sarcastic wave with his hand that was holding a cordless microphone. The co-ordinator shook her head in derision and to make matters worse, an arm dropped off the nearest dummy.

The third terrace was filled with dense smoke, the sort of smoke that comes from a machine. The co-ordinator led them onto the terrace with her shrill voice cutting through the theatrical smoke.

'This is the terrace of the wrathful...' the co-ordinator began; but Jennifer had had enough of the tour and wanted to get away. She grabbed Evan by the arm and led him from the party and to an area where the smoke was thinner.

'Where are we going?' Evan asked.

'Away from her,' she said.

'Oh right. I guess it was a bit disappointing.'

'I'd rather be at a wake.'

'So, what do you want to do?'

'I don't know. Wait, let's go up to the fourth terrace.'

'But that's off limits,' Evan said.

'Exactly,' she said.

They felt their way toward the steps that led up to the fourth terrace. The smoke thinned as they crested onto a terrace made of flint. It was so quiet: the noise of the group was now completely gone.

'Are you sure we should be up here?' Evan said.

'What are you afraid of? We've got a while before the group heads back to the ship. Come over here and sit down with me,' Jennifer said sitting down cross legged with her back to the sheer rock face that rose above them.

'How did you die?' Jennifer asked once they were both settled.

'I'd rather not say,' Evan replied cagily.

'It can't be that bad, come on tell me. If it helps, I'll tell you how I died: I was walking back from the library with a few books that I'd been meaning to read,' Jennifer explained, 'I went to cross the road, but my books started to tumble, so I just kept on walking, into the path of a bus. Silly really.'

'No, sounds...normal.'

'Soo...how?' she said.

'You'll just laugh.'

'I promise I won't.'

'I choked to death on a Ginger Nut biscuit,' he said frankly.

Jennifer burst out laughing, 'Sorry I didn't mean to. How did you manage that? I mean they're quite big, aren't they?'

Evan shrugged, 'I think my reason for existence was purely to prove that it is possible to choke to death on a Ginger Nut.'

'Important work, very important.'

They heard the steps of someone approaching from further along the terrace ledge.

'Who is this on my terrace?' the angel boomed in a croaky voice.

They both stood up quickly and recoiled from the advancing angel. His robe was no longer brilliant white, but rather soiled putty with odd brown stains. He had a long grey beard that was heavily matted with grease and the sword that he levelled at them with great effort was pitted with rust all the way to the hilt.

'We're just part of the tour. We got lost,' Jennifer said quickly.

'The tour? What tour?' the angel said lowering his sword - to lean on.

'The tour of Mount Purgatory.'

'They do tours now?'

'Only the first three terraces, they don't allow anyone to go higher.'

'First I've heard of it. But then again, I've not left my terrace in five centuries. After Heaven closed the mountain down, the council invited us back to Heaven.' He coughed out his bronchi, causing some wing feathers to flutter off. 'Out of the nine angels guarding the seven levels of the mountain, five returned. Four of us decided to stay upon the mountain, to protect it from the agents of evil. Out of respect for its timeless heritage, we sought to prevent this sacred mountain from being over-run with demons. You are the first people I have seen or spoken to since that time.'

'Which terrace is this?' Jennifer asked.

'This is the terrace for the slothful,' the angel said, giving Evan a long stare. 'You wouldn't like it here boy.'

Evan visibly shrunk from him. 'I think we should go,' Evan pleaded.

They made their way back down the terraces and met up with the group back on the beach where the passengers were putting their lifejackets back on and climbing back into the angel's boat. Once they were all on board the pilot angel spread his impressive wingspan to catch the ether's energy waves and they were off, back to the ship.

The Void

The next day Evan was constantly thinking about Jennifer. He wandered through the various lounges and public areas of the ship in a thoughtful daze. He walked up the wide, elegant central stairway, up to the starboard promenade deck.

The deck was dark but drew in some light from the cabin lights of the ship. Evan had to remind himself that he wasn't standing on a normal cruise liner deck at night, but was aboard Purgatory, which was enveloped by the blackness of the inter-dimensional ether at all hours.

A high-pitched wailing sound came from the direction of the stern. It stopped and then carried on but a little louder. A naked old man rounded the corner of the stern about a hundred meters from where Evan had emerged and was running down the length of the starboard side. It was the same elderly man who had made an exhibition of himself in the Mezzanine bar two days earlier, during Gerard's sales pitch. The man had found himself another nautical hat. Two crew members were behind him, in pursuit: their boots making a hollow thwack upon the wooden deck. The man's wailing began to become discernible as words: 'I've paid my taxes! I've paid my purging tax! I can run naked if I want to! Do you hear? Naked like Adam! I run into the arms of my maker!'

'Stop him! Trip him up!' the lead crew member shouted to Evan. Evan didn't move; the man stopped and turned to Evan.

'Remember,' he said, 'we were all born naked and so it is that we must be naked in our death. They have no power over me; my own inner conscience is the only authority that guides my life: a conscience that is guided by God himself.'

'I think they're gaining on you,' Evan said pointing to the slow but steady progress of the puffing crew.

He started off in the direction of the bow; before he got far, another crew member had come from the front of the ship, to cut off his escape. He backtracked and tried to open one of the doors, but it was locked; the nautical hat was taken from him, dusted off and apologetically returned to the officer it belonged to.

Evan shrugged, walked over to the railings and looked down the side of the ship. There was no water line, just the hull sloping inward to meet the other side of the ship in the black void. A shoal of jellyfish went past, pulsating their translucent bodies in phase with one another as if they were one organism, controlled by some great cosmic mind.

'Hello dear boy,' Derek said as he floated past Evan on the outside of the ship. The drunkard was reclined on his back with his hands comfortably folded behind his hairy head. His smelly tweed jacket was undone and fell away from his portly belly, with a stained string vest underneath. He had a half-full pint of beer balanced on his stomach. Evan tracked him with astonished eyes as he levitated past at eye level, outside of the hull, suspended in the black ether.

'What the...?' Evan managed. 'How? Is that you Derek?'

'It's really me. The dead me anyway.'

'What are you doing in the ether?'

'Going for a float,' he replied. Derek unhooked a hand, reached forward and took a swig of beer, before carefully replacing it in the well grooved drink receptacle crater around his belly button, made from displaced fat. The two friends began to drift apart due to the forward motion of the ship. Derek staying still in the ether, whilst the ship slowly ground its way toward Heaven. 'Walk with me,' Derek invited.

'But you're not walking.'

'You know what I mean. Walk while I float. You can be so argumentative.'

'Isn't it against the rules to float around in the ether?'

'Yes, it's against the rules, but I find it relaxing.'

'If a crew member comes, I'll pull you in to save you any trouble.'

'No need my boy: all of the crew on this side of the ship are busy with Mr Naked Running Man, so I took the opportunity to go for a float.'

'What was wrong with him?' Evan asked his levitating friend.

'Some people find it difficult to adjust to the afterlife surroundings. I guess a mixture of confusion, stress and denial sends them over the edge into madness.'

'Did you ever go mad?'

'In my early days, but then I found that the soothing effects of alcohol. I must say that you're bearing up well for a new boy; what's your secret?' the floating Derek asked.

'Complacency I guess.'

Derek ran an idle hand through his mop of brown hair. 'What have you been up to, haven't seen you in a while?'

'I met girl. Jennifer.' Evan said.

'Do you want my advice?' Derek offered.

'No.'

'Fine. Come on in, the ether's fine and sublime,' he encouraged.

'I can't, you know that I can't break the rules.'

'Just have a quick go, so that you can say you've done it. It might even impress what's-her-name?'

'Jennifer.'

Against his better judgement, Evan decided to give it a go. He zipped his blue waterproof jacket up tight, grabbed the railings and went to hop over.

'WAIT,' Derek ordered. 'You have to lie flat, or you'll sink like a stone: the ether is just dense enough to hold a person lying down.'

'How did you work that one out?' Evan asked as he gently lowered himself horizontally along the outside of the railings.

'In my long years aboard, I've seen many people jumping off the railings of this ship and into the ether because they couldn't stand the purging sessions and had heard that Heaven wasn't all they hoped it would be.'

'You mean suicide.'

'The fools probably thought that they were going to somehow fall to their death. Of course, they forgot that they were already dead. The truth is that they just end up falling through the ether for eternity. Unless they work out how to lie flat. In which case, they end up floating in the ether for eternity, some suicide. I started experimenting with pancakes, lifted from the buffet restaurant. Once fully spread, they were able to float in the ether. Even with various toppings of sugar, jam, boysenberries etc added to the top surface, they would remain suspended...'

'So, they're still out there somewhere?' Evan said as a shiver went down his spine at the prospect of someone spending an eternity in this featureless black void.

'I expect so yes. Best not to think about it boy, or else you'll end up going mad, like Mr Naked Running Man.'

Derek's beer gently slopped around in his glass with each of his deep slow breaths. Evan was on the inside, right next to the outer railings, being ready to grab it should the ether suddenly give way underneath him. A breeze began to pick up causing the hood and tassels of Evan's waterproof to flutter against his body.

'Should we be unfortunate enough to experience a rogue wave...' Derek said.

'I felt a breeze just now. Does that matter?'

'A breeze is usually caused by inter-dimensional friction which is usually the precursor to energy waves. So yes, it does matter, and for prudence's sake we should probably get back on board before...WAVE! GET OUT!' Derek cried as he pointed to a large energy wave barrelling its way toward them.

In his hurry to get back over the railings and clear the way for his friend who was further out, Evan broke the golden rule of ether floating and instinctively dropped his legs vertically. He instantly began to fall. He managed to get a precarious grip on the wooden deck of the ship, where the bottom of the railings finished, and the outer hull began. Derek was starting to curse loudly as he swam toward the deck to get out of the wave's path and rescue his floundering young friend.

'Hold on my boy! I'll be there in a second!'

Evan's fingertip grip was starting to slide. Just as Derek landed heavily of the deck and dashed to his aid, the waxy deck polish won the day. Evan lost his grip and plummeted down into the blackness.

Evan realised that he was still falling through the ether, and so flicked his legs back and arms forward to make himself into a human pancake. He started to decelerate, with the ether streaming around his body, plastering his clothes to his front, and billowing his cheeks. Soon enough, he was perfectly still, suspended in the eerie, silent darkness.

He rolled over onto his back, careful to do it quickly and splay his limbs to stop himself falling any further. Not that it would help him: he was now adrift and alone in the ether with no chance of rescue. He looked up and saw the lights of Purgatory way above him, moving steadily away.

Feelings of despondency, regret and short pangs of fear gripped him as he floated alone. It was only then that he realised that his greatest fear was that of being completely unmissed. Like the quiet person at a party who feels swamped out of occasion by the more outgoing people, who slopes off early, wondering if anyone from the party will miss them as they walk home on the quiet streets of some uncaring city. Derek would miss him for a little while, but after a few weeks of drinking, Evan would just be a hazy memory that would be put down to a trick of the imagination. Jennifer also may think of him now and then, but he would soon be forgotten once she got to Heaven and met someone else. Everyone he had ever known on Earth would die someday and everyone in the afterlife would move on. There would be no one to remember his laziness or strange sense of humour. No one to think kindly or even ill of him. In some ways he would have preferred it if, out there somewhere, he had an eternal nemesis that spent all his time hating Evan and plotting to find him and destroy him. At least it would give his existence external meaning.

His thoughts turned to Jennifer; that possibility was now out of his grasp. He lapsed into a fantasy of the two of them living happily together in Heaven. Of course, Evan realised that it may not have worked out like that, but these thoughts were all that kept him from insanity.

Purgatory was a faint glow of light, way off. He imagined the guilt that Derek better be feeling for getting him into this mess. He thought of Derek's hairy, untidy face and realised that his would be the last human face that he would ever see. In some ways he wished that it was Jennifer who had invited him to join her for a float along the starboard railings rather than his scruffy friend.

A jellyfish languidly pulsated up to him, as if to investigate the new addition to the ether. Evan tried to stroke it, but stroking a jellyfish is not like stroking a cat; the slimy malleable surface did not comfort him. Then he cursed himself: not only was the last human face he would see, Derek's, but now the last living creature he would ever touch was a jellyfish. He closed his eyes and drifted off with tears in his eyes.

The Lonely Jellyfish Herder

Evan was woken up by a hand gently shaking his shoulder; he sleepily opened his eyes. At first, he thought that he had gone blind: there was complete blackness. He blinked furiously, rubbed his eyes and looked wildly around him, but there was nothing. Disparate strands of thought all collided with one another as he remembered where he was.

'No! No! NO!' he screamed. The phantom hand shook him again and Evan realised that it was coming from below.

'Is everything alright?' the voice asked, with chirpy concern. Evan twisted his head to look below, but his neck would not stretch far enough to see the voice bearer. He did a quick barrel roll and stopped with his stomach facing down and his limbs splayed out like a star. The first thing that grabbed his attention was the vast shoal of jellyfish stretched out below him like an immense, white, fleshy carpet. They were all pulsating and moving together off to the right. He then turned his attention to the angel that was talking to him. He was gaunt faced and sickly looking, as if he had never been exposed to sunlight. He was wearing white clothing: it reminded Evan of Samurai armour, the type that was made from interlocked leather, hemp and bronze; except that the angel's was made from tatty white cloth. His garb had deteriorated to the state where the interlocked linen had worked loose all over his body and now flapped and streamed in the ether breeze. The angel was astride a dolphin, lightly handling its reigns.

'No, I'm not alright,' Evan replied.

The angel pulled back on the reins to hold back his dolphin steed from moving on. The dolphin looked irritable at the break from its journey; but once the weathered angel leaned forward and gently rubbed its smooth head, it quietened down and began to lazily swish its tail.

'So which jellyfish does he want terminated?' the angel asked with a heavy heart.

'No, you don't understand, I fell off Purgatory.'

'Oh right...Nice weather we've been having?' the angel said.

Evan looked at the angel in confusion, wondering how the state of any weather had any bearing on the situation. The angel looked down, almost guiltily.

'Who are you? Are you my guardian angel?' Evan asked.

'No,' The angel replied, 'I have been denied such fulfilling tasks as being a guardian angel. I'm not allowed to sing in the Heavenly Host either; or play the harp which is really annoying because I was just getting good - grade six.'

The angel looked down again, but in moroseness. He leaned forward to stroke the dolphin's head, taking comfort from the benign presence of the mammal, then turned the leather reigns idly in his hand. 'No, I'm not a proper angel any longer, but one of a few jellyfish herders that tend to the shoals that migrate across the ether.'

'Good job is it?' Evan asked.

The jellyfish herder looked at him with grey, unmerry eyes.

'It's not the busiest stand at the careers fair.'

'Why do you do it then?'

'I was cast out of Heaven after the great battle, for not taking sides. God was in no mood for sympathy; me and a few other angels who were undecided while the battle against Satan, and the other rebel angels raged, were cast out of Heaven to spend the rest of eternity herding and tending to the jellyfish, as punishment for our lack of conviction.'

'I'm sorry,' Evan said. 'So how about that lift back to Purgatory then?'

'You don't want to stay for a bit of a chat first?' the herder asked tentatively. 'I don't get much company out here in the ether, so it's nice to have a bit of a chat when I do come across people.' He laughed in a desperate sort of way. 'You know stops the old grey cells turning to mush.'

There was an uncomfortable silence and then the herder coughed then spoke.

'So, nice whether we've been having?'

'What are all of these jellyfish doing in the ether? And why are they the only animals around?' Evan asked forthrightly.

'I'm really not supposed to tell.'

'I'll talk to you for a whole hour,' Evan offered.

The lonely herder thought about this and then nodded in affirmation.

'You have a deal, but no drifting off and pretending to be listening when you're not. I really don't like it when people do that.'

The herder cleared his throat and arranged the reigns neatly over one another in his left hand, using his right hand to indicate his flock of migrating jellyfish beneath them. 'The jellyfish are a control mechanism over people in the afterlife. You see, even when people get to Heaven, they still possess free will, which can lead to wrongdoing. God could not abide the thought of people committing serious crimes in Heaven, nor could he abide the unsavoury spectacle of punishing people in paradise. So, he created the jellyfish solution. The life force of both the individual and their jellyfish are completely dependent on one another. If one dies, then so does the other. If someone commits a mortal sin whilst in paradise, a jellyfish finder team are sent out from Heaven to track down the appropriate jellyfish – and terminate it. They usually liaise with us herders on account of our intimate knowledge of our shoals. This also answers your second question about why they are the only animals in the ether, because they are not really animals as such, just pseudo souls that happen to take the form of an Earthen jellyfish.' The herder shifted to a more comfortable position on the back of his dolphin. 'Now we will converse for one hour,' he stated. 'First I will recant to you my early memories as a young angel growing up in the bosom of The Almighty...times were blissful back then; Earth had yet to be created; the angels danced and sang; harps were played with little thought about the dire events that would unfold. Naturally, there was no time back then, The Almighty had not created it, so I guess you could say that I have no idea of how old I am - what a strange concept...'

'...And that is my current opinion on the viability of using waste agricultural matter in the production of domestic plant pots.'

The dolphin let out a loud, distressed bark, clearly not being able to take any more.

'Was that an hour already? Never mind, got the larynx juices flowing.'

The jellyfish herder stood up in his stirrups, folded the dolphin's dorsal fin to one side, moved himself over it and sat heavily on the front side of the fin that had popped back up behind him; before pulling the stirrups forward and placing his boots back into them. The dolphin yacked in protest because the herder was now sitting on his blowhole. The herder apologised and shifted back a bit. Evan carefully manoeuvred his hovering body until he was over the back of the dolphin. He flicked himself vertical and landed, legs either side of the dolphin, very nearly losing his balance on the smooth skin of the mammal. The herder whipped his reigns and the dolphin accelerated off in the direction of Purgatory.

The dolphin beat its tail quickly, causing its whole back to arch and straighten in a constant cycle. Evan held onto the herder's tatty white attire to stop himself being flicked off.

Performing a skilful skid stop, the herder's steed came along side Purgatory, so that it lay swishing abreast of the port side railings, keeping pace with the ship as it moved steadily forward.

'Thanks for the ride...'

'Ezekiel is my name.'

'Thank you, you really saved me back there.'

'It was a pleasure, and any time you want another chat...'

'Bye...um...Mr Dolphin,' Evan hazarded.

'No, no, he doesn't like that.'

The dolphin chattered something.

'He says that "Mr Dolphin" is too broad a concept. It tends to lump all dolphins together into an adorable, generic identity.'

The dolphin nodded its smooth head.

'What *does* he like to be called?' Evan asked.

The dolphin chattered excitedly and made a chopping motion with his side fin.

'At the moment he responds to, "The ninja pirate ether being".'

Evan patted the dolphin's head, 'He's certainly not a conformist.'

The herder fiddled with his reigns again.

'I suppose I'd better get back to my shoal, otherwise the little beggars start to form large geometric shapes. It was nice to talk to you though....'

'Evan.'

With that the jellyfish herder flicked his reigns, dug in his heels and shot off into the darkness straddling his rebellious dolphin.

The Purging Deck

Evan went in search of Derek to give him a prolonged throttling for persuading him to go ether floating. He sat down at the nearest bar stool and ordered a double vodka and coke, then told the barman to go easy on the coke, before asking him to put in an extra shot of vodka. Evan realised that he was ravenously hungry due to all the worry he had gone through stranded in the ether. He lifted his body, stretching an arm across the bar top to pull a bowl of peanuts toward him. After snuffling the entire content of the bowl and licking the residual salt, he drank his strong tonic in two wincing gulps.

'Busy shift?' Evan asked the barman. The jellyfish herder had no doubt rubbed off on him. The barman smiled warmly, shook his head, but carried on buffing a glass. Evan ordered a half of cider to mellow the hit of spirit.

'How long have you been here?' the barman asked as he swiped Evan's cabin card through the register.

'You mean how long have I been dead?' Evan said. The barman nodded.

'Three days,' Evan answered, 'and you?'

The barman tilted his head slightly, 'Four months.'

'I guess that it isn't what you expected: having to spend eternity working as a barman on Purgatory.'

The barman looked confused.

'No, I am not dead. I am on a six-month contract; I get purging absolution for me and my family when we die.' The barman said and then nodded to Evan before recommencing with his glass buffing duties.

He passed the empty glass back to the barman and walked out of the Mezzanine Bar to scour the ship for the drunkard. It was coming up to lunchtime, and so Evan started by going to the self-service, buffet bar. The long metal tray rails snaked along a whole side of the room in front of the hotplates that were laden with hot foods: Lasagne, cottage pie, sausages and other Westernised dishes. An elderly woman was pushing her tray along the rails, mechanically scooping food on to her plate. Evan scanned the seating area, which was made up of cheap wooded chairs and wipe clean tabletops. There were about a dozen people quietly munching on their lunch. They were spread out all over the large seating area, like an under subscribed old people's home. He had come here first because he knew that Derek had an adversity to the formal, silver service restaurant at the other end of the ship.

Evan knocked on Derek's cabin door, but no answer; he scanned the Auditorium on the fifth deck, in case Derek was sprawled out on the floor in a boozy slumber. He wasn't and so Evan checked out the small cinema on the same deck; then the Outlook Lounge on the seventh deck. He wandered back down to the fifth deck and walked along the full length of the wooden promenades that went all the way around the ship, finally bounding up the external staircase on the bow of the ship up to the Sun Deck; but he was nowhere to be found. Evan slumped down in one of the many recliners arranged around the edges and wondered where his friend was.

His recent brush with complete abandonment in the ether had given him new confidence and curiosity. Evan decided to sneak a look at the purging deck and see for himself what this ship was all about.

He walked through the French windows, through the bar and out to the main stairway in the centre of the ship. He went down through the intermediary decks and slowed as he approached the first deck. The red carpeted area in front of the stairway was just like any other part of the ship; with a highly polished chrome rail along the side walls, an extravagant chandelier hanging from the ceiling. Christian and nautical paintings adorning the magnolia walls, as well as a map of the lay-out of the ship bolted on the wall. The only difference was a single functional wooden door that faced opposite the stairs. The door was labelled "Purging suites". Evan stood and listened but couldn't hear anything. He pushed open the door and went in.

Behind the door lay a long, utilitarian corridor. Hard wearing brown carpet squares were illuminated by electric strip lights. There were doorways off the dingy corridor all the way as far as Evan could see, on both the right and the left. He went to the first door on the left that read "stretching rack suite 1" The next door read "recovery room."

He pressed his ear to the door of "stretching rack suite 1" and listened. He could hear something, but it was very quiet. Evan imagined a horrific scene; images of a Medieval torture chamber flooded his mind. He braced himself and peeped in. The first thing he noticed was the lack of Medieval equipment in the room. It was just like an office function room with neutral walls and carpet. The next thing he noticed was the television set on top of a chair. He then realised that the noise was coming from a television set. Pushing the door fully open, he became very confused. There were about fifteen people around the television, sitting on plastic chairs, watching the screen. Some of them, he recognised as being the staff, who were smoking cigarettes. The grey smoke wisps lazily culminating above their black-haired heads. Derek was on the end of the semicircle silently watching the screen. Evan walked quietly into the room and pulled up a chair next to his friend.

'What's going on?' Evan whispered.

'Just watching a bit of "Crime Scene Investigation",' the drunkard replied.

Derek pulled his attention away from the screen to see who was talking to him.

'Evan my boy! You're back! I thought I'd lost you.'

One of the staff, Edwardo, leaned forward in his chair and politely asked them to be quiet.

'Yes, I'm back,' Evan whispered. 'Why are you watching CSI?'

'We watch it every week, we're halfway through season three. Edwardo over there brought in the boxset: he's a bit of a fan,' Derek said at normal volume. 'Not really my cup of tea but I guess you can't have everything. How did you get out of the ether?'

'I got a lift with a jellyfish herder on the back of his dolphin,' Evan stated. 'I didn't mean why you are watching CSI specifically; I meant, why are you watching television on the purging deck, instead of being purged?'

'Please be quiet,' Edwardo hissed.

'Since when do jellyfish herders ride around on dolphins? And why didn't I know that?' Derek said irritably, not liking that his young friend knew something that he didn't.

'I may, someday, enlighten you to the finer workings of the afterlife,' Evan said loftily. 'So, you're all bunking off?'

'Yes,' Derek said, ignoring the glares coming from Edwardo, whilst pointing to the side of the room, where some man-sized metallic stretching racks had been pushed out of the way. 'We're supposed to be on those things but hardly anyone checks up on us. Plus, it's a welcome break for the staff.'

The telephone began to ring. Edwardo got up reluctantly and answered it. He only listened for a brief time and then put down the receiver.

'Maggie Richards is on her way down,' he announced to the room. Everyone in the purging suite knew what this meant, staff and passengers alike. Someone wheeled away the television, unplugged it and pushed it into a cupboard. The chairs were quickly stacked on one another and pushed into the corner. Then the stretching racks were wheeled back into the centre of the room. The passengers jumped up onto them and began to strap themselves down with Velcro flaps. Evan just watched from the side-lines, not knowing what to do. Derek grabbed him and put him on a rack, telling him to stay still and not say anything, before mounting his own rack.

Maggie Richards, the purging supervisor, opened the door and swished into the room wearing a two-piece pinstripe suit and a business-like expression. As soon as the door had opened, the passengers started to make horrendous noises of suffering. The staff stood by the stretching racks and pretended to be inputting the correct amount of pressure into the digital rack-side computers.

'Everything alright Edwardo?' Maggie asked.

'Yes, yes,' Edwardo enthused, 'a successful session of purging Mrs Richards.'

She ticked something on a clipboard.

'Everything seems to be in order, I shall let you get on with it.'

The hastily hidden television fell out of the cupboard with a crack as it hit the floor.

'Why is there a television down here Edwardo?' Maggie asked.

Edwardo floundered and began to sweat. Derek sat up on his rack, then remembered that he was supposed to be strapped down, and so lay back down.

'Edwardo showed us a safety video about the possible dangers of the purging process before the session started,' he said.

'I wasn't aware that there was a video?' Maggie said, listening to Derek, but still looking at Edwardo, who was crumbling under her stern gaze.

'Oh yes,' Derek continued, 'health and safety: we should all be wearing protective goggles and hair nets.'

Maggie turned to Derek, his eyes emanating the pure mastery of lying.

'Very well, I shall see what we can do.' She turned on her heels and exited the purging suite.

They all let out murmurs of relief as the door swung shut.

'Like a well-oiled machine, well done everyone,' Derek said. 'Apart from Edwardo of course, who buckled like super-heated steel.'

Edwardo gave him a disdainful look. 'It wasn't my fault that the television fell out of the cupboard,' he sulked.

'Yes, but you didn't exactly stand your ground with Maggie back there, did you? You should learn to bury your mild-mannered culture now and again.'

'Shut up Derek!' he said.

'That's the spirit!'

The Captain's Dinner Party

The next morning, a small pamphlet was slid underneath Evan's cabin door. He walked over and picked up the latest edition of "cruise news". He sat down and glanced at the front page which was dominated by one article - the Captain's Dinner Party. It was being held at seven o'clock that night and was a compulsory event. The dress code was strictly black tie. Evan panicked, quickly got up and opened the wardrobe and sure enough there was a crisp and clean dinner suit hanging there for him.

He met Derek in the Mezzanine Bar. It was eleven o'clock and just opening.

'Seems to get later every day I swear,' he grumbled and wasted no time in ordering the first drinks of the day. 'What brings you out of your pit so early? Usually, you're dead to the world until midday, if you'll excuse the pun.'

'This came through the door.'

'Oh, the dreaded Captain's Dinner Party; it's come around already has it,' he sighed, then banged his fists down on the bar, disrupting a bowl of peanuts. 'Why me! Every bloody week of every bloody year, why, why!' he exclaimed tearing at his mop of unwashed hair.

'It can't be that bad surely?'

'The other strange people on the ship actually enjoy themselves and have a great time,' he said, 'but they haven't been to it thirty-three years on the trot, have they? Plus, I had a very depressing revelation recently.'

'What, that you've eaten enough food at them to feed a small African country for a year?' Evan suggested.

'No; but thank you for adding to my spiral of self-loathing,' Derek cleared his throat, 'I have, in fact had more bodily contact with the captain of this ship than a pair of new lovers.'

Evan was shocked. 'Derek. I think that's really brave of you. I'm truly honoured that you've decided to share your sexuality with me. I mean it must be difficult for a man of your...manner...to come forth with something like that.'

'No, you idiot!' he said smacking Evan across the face with the back of his hand. 'The fact is: I've had to shake hands with the sod every week on the way into dinner for thirty-three years!'

Evan nursed his jaw with an ice pack the attentive bar tender had produced.

'Do you know what? I think I prefer you when you're drunk.'

'Sorry, I'm not a morning person,' Derek said in a detached voice.

'Well neither am I, but I don't go around smacking people for no reason; and even if I were so inclined, I'd have the common courtesy to stay in bed until the urge had passed,' Evan chastised.

After a silence and a quick depletion of his pint glass, Derek turned to Evan.

'You're bringing your girlfriend then?'

'I haven't asked her yet.'

'Well, I'd hurry up if I were you, the competition's pretty stiff. I mean I know that ninety-five percent of them are over fifty but I'm sure there's the odd dark horse amongst them,' he jibed.

'Stop making me paranoid. She'll go with me, I'm sure of it. Let's face it. I'm the only passenger under the age of thirty, so it's pretty much in the bag.'

'You old romantic. Is that how you plan to woo her affections? By waiting for the perfect moment to whisper gently into her ear, "you know I'm the only guy on the ship your age, how about it?"'

'Not exactly no. Are you coming?'

'Yes. No way out of it. Well, that's not entirely true; I once got so desperate that I hid in the exhaust funnel. Thought it was a brilliant idea until I realised that in order not to appear as "missing" on the dinner roster, I had stay in it for a whole week, only coming out to lick condensation off the hand railings.'

'So that's a yes then?'

'Yes, that's a yes. But don't expect me to enjoy myself or "big you up" in front of...what's-her-name.'

'Jennifer.'

'Jennifer. Don't expect me to tell her of the time you worked with blind children or subtly mention about how massive your member is.'

'Fine, just don't put her off by acting like a cretin. You know what they say about judging people by their friends.'

'What, don't, because people usually hang out with people they consider to be morons to make themselves feel better about themselves.'

'Great Derek, is that why you hang out with me is it?'

'Hang out with you? You're always following me around.'

'How could anybody possibly follow you around?! You're always sat right there in that stool, in this bar, every single day!'

'What's your point?' Derek asked cagily.

'I'm just saying, it wouldn't hurt if you got out a bit more, met new people, met a new lady friend maybe,' he added more softly.

'Look just because you've got lucky, doesn't mean you have a licence to rub into my nose like a tissue full of excrement. And anyway, what's the point: If hypothetically I did meet the love of my life here, she would only be around for a week and then she'd be off to Heaven, leaving me behind in Purgatory to feel all lovelorn and depressed.'

'You're already depressed.'

'You sound like my second wife.'

'Why did she leave?'

'None of your business.'

'Anyway, we'll meet here at six o'clock, yes?'

'Yes dear.'

'Look I'm not your bloody second wife you miserable old bastard!' Evan exploded.

'Looks like someone should have had the common courtesy to stay in bed,' Derek replied calmly.

'Six then?' Evan continued now calm again.

'With bells on.' He thought of adding "dear" on the end as Evan was walking away but decided not to – the boy was coming along well and he didn't want to shake his confidence, especially with a new girl to impress.

They were sitting at the bar in the Mezzanine Bar discussing how ridiculous they both looked in their dinner jackets, when a red motion caught the corner of Evan's eye.

He swivelled his head to see Jennifer walking toward them from the stairwell entrance. Evan reckoned that he had put some effort into his appearance for tonight, but it paled in comparison to the lengths it must have taken her to individually curl each part of her hair. When it was straight it was an asset to her, but now loosely curled and full of life as she moved, it took on new meanings of fiery uncontrollability.

The full-length red dress hugged her body perfectly, and as she walked, the single long slit down the side revealed her athletic legs. Evan's jaw almost dropped to the floor.

She swished majestically to the bar and smiled at the dithering Evan. Derek stood up and violently poked him until he did likewise.

'Good evening my dear,' Derek said in an articulate civilised manner. They both looked at him.

'Oh, right. Derek, this is Jennifer. Jennifer, Derek,' She offered Derek her hand and he lightly kissed it.

'Would you like a drink?' Evan said pulling a stool out for her to sit on. She placed her handbag on the bar and slid onto the seat with minimal rearrangement.

'Yes, a martini please.'

'You look very nice.' Evan cautiously stated.

'Thank you very much.'

Derek sensed that an awkward silence was about to creep up on the young pair and so he intervened.

'Have you been to a Captain's Dinner before Jennifer?' He asked politely.

'No, I can't say I have.'

'Well then, tonight will be a night to remember!' he burst out with a great big smile and a merry laugh, contorting his hairy face.

She giggled and then gently caressed one of Evan's fingers, down low between their bodies, where Derek could not see. Evan quickly looked at her face to see if it was accidental or deliberate, but she didn't give anything away. His heart was still fluttering after they'd finished the first round of drinks.

After making it through the sausage machine that was the captain's handshake procession, the three of them made their way with the rest of the smartly dressed passengers to the dining hall.

'Three please Joseph.' Derek said to the waiter.

'Good evening, Mr Derek. You've company tonight?'

'Yes, well, strange things happen at sea.'

'Please follow me,' he gestured with his arm.

They arrived at a table for six, which was already occupied by three strangers. Evan and Jennifer sat opposite each other at one end of the table; Derek sat in the middle next to Jennifer and opposite a woman; with the other end of the table being occupied by another couple. All six of them wasted no time in ordering drinks.

Astonishingly Derek reigned in his instinct to order three for himself, so instead ordered a triple whiskey as a compromise. After some general pleasantries the starters arrived.

'Well, my wife and I have been very impressed by the service so far. The ship is excellent and so professionally run – a tight ship if you will...'

'Ha,' Derek burbled, 'About as tight as the captain's handshake!' The single woman who had introduced herself as Susan tried desperately to hide a smirk. The man glared at Derek for the interruption. Derek made a weak gesture of apology.

'...It really does beat most of the cruises we experienced on back on Earth, don't you think dear?'

'Oh definitely,' They were obviously two of a kind, 'And the Filipino staff are just sooo friendly, it's like they actually love to serve us. Not like those abrasive Eastern Europeans – dreadful people, which one was that Charles?'

'Mediterranean Magic.'

'Oh yes – dreadful.'

Derek took a sip of whisky and very quickly winked at the woman opposite. After her small indiscretion, he guessed that she was on his side and would probably back him up for the childish fun he was about to have with the prudish couple next to them. What he was about to do wasn't big or clever and deep down he disliked himself for doing it. It was however one of his few avenues of pleasure in his otherwise routine and hazy existence aboard Purgatory.

'And what brings you here?' Derek asked the couple. They looked at each other in confusion and then the man – Charles, answered.

'Well, we died.'

'Oh dear; how unfortunate for you both. Nothing serious I hope?' He smiled pleasantly.

'No, no, I don't think you understand we DIED,' Charles stated.

'What; both at the same time? How curious. Do you mind me asking what of? – No wait,' he raised his fingers to his temples like a clairvoyant, 'you both ate from the same tin of salmon mousse.' Both Susan and Evan got the Monty Python reference and laughed through closed mouths, forcing the sound to grate in their throats. Jennifer gave Evan a quizzical look, so he made a "tell you later" gesture which she understood.

'No,' The man said slightly defensively, 'We died in a fire, our house burnt down in the night, and we asphyxiated in our sleep.'

'Well, if it makes you feel better, there have been many studies to show that being burnt alive in your sleep is the most peaceful way to go,' Derek said with mock sympathy.

Susan looked up from her crab salad, 'And it saves on cremation fees.'

Derek smiled. It was a smile that Evan had not seen before, a small and subtle smile, not the usual manic contortion of facial muscles.

Derek decided to back off the couple just for a bit. He was just warming up but didn't want to lose them just yet.

The starter plates were cleared away to the sound of the couple's constant nattering about the usual topics of acceptable conversation, such as: Which players had been seeded for Wimbledon; how they were planning to reduce their "carbon footprint"; and that for a wine which was endorsed by Heaven, it was "really quite dreadful".

Derek couldn't hold it in any longer, the bloody woman had used the word "dreadful" too many times, and one of the many things that got on Derek's wick was people too lazy to vary their vocabulary.

'If you find the wine unsatisfactory, I can highly recommend the single malt, you never know, it might give you a bit more flavour,' Derek said.

Charles scowled at him.

'I mean, you might find it more flavoursome,' he quickly added and then cleared his throat. 'Are you a whiskey man Charles?'

'I'm not a drinker on the whole.'

'Why's that, medical reasons?'

'Religious.'

'Buddhists, are you? Do you know, I had a hunch you might have been?'

'No, I'm not a Buddhist.'

'Fundamental Islamist?'

'Christian.'

'Yes, of course, I do apologise, I sometimes forget where we are. Funnily enough, I did know a Buddhist on the ship. Don't ask me how he got on board...'

'Must have stowed away?' Susan suggested.

'...Yes, you're probably right. They've got him scrubbing toilets now, for eternity. I guess it serves him right, for choosing not to put complete faith in a deity – the little beggar.'

'Gosh that's terrible,' Charles' wife gasped, swallowing the story hook line and sinker.

'Yes, indeed, poor man. He's now completely convinced that he'll be reincarnated as the toilet duck.'

The main course arrived.

Charles sensed that they were both being used as the butt of dinner conversation, and decided it was probably a better idea to concentrate on his food than invite another bout of humiliation at the hands of the hairy heathen. His wife on the other hand blundered on regardless, seemingly oblivious to fun being made at her expense.

'Of course, this isn't a stitch to some of the charity dinners we've been to. Isn't that right Charles?'

'Mrmm,' He had decided to cut the cord and let his wife fall alone.

'Like, the "African Charitable Trust", do you remember that one? Oh, talk about grandeur, and the service impeccable. They could take a leaf out of that book here, that's for sure.'

'Sorry, what was that charity again?' Derek enquired.

'The "African Charitable Trust",' She repeated, except a bit louder in the hope that the neighbouring table might overhear.

'And what do they do?'

She was well prepared for such a question; after all, it wasn't the first time that she had slipped it into dinner time conversation.

'It's a charitable organisation which acts as mediation between the many other charities and Non-Governmental Organisations that operate on the African continent.'

'Like a coordinating influence?' Susan said interested.

'Exactly, making sure that vital knowledge is shared and that schemes don't overlap and such forth.'

'A worthy cause if I may say so,' Derek said to stall for time in order to find the right angle of attack. This one after all was a real challenge for him. She had the social equivalent of a full house, whereas he was scratching around with a low pair: Time to bluff.

'And a cause very close to my heart,' Derek suddenly announced.

Susan gave him a worried "don't you dare" look, which he ignored.

'Yes, I spent many years on the continent in my younger days with the United Nations Development Programme,' Derek said.

Susan's pupils dilated.

'We had to deal with the various development organisations of the time,' Derek continued, 'complete chaos of course, no funding available, and the institutional infrastructure was so scant, that it was almost impossible to get anything done.'

'Yes, it was terrible in those days,' Charles' wife said overly confidently. Derek saw his angle.

'I suppose it's all change since this charity was established?'

'Oh yes, I'm sure with all the new coordination, the situation is definitely improving.'

'A lot of new changes on the continent though that must be hard to deal with. How is the Trust dealing with North Coast Immigration problem?' Derek asked, wondering whether she would take the bait.

'The...what?'

'The NCI - the North Coast Immigration problem - a terrible drain on Africa's resources. Did you know that over twenty thousand Eastern European migrants arrive on the shores of Morocco, Algeria and Tunisia every day?!'

'But aren't they going to Western Europe?' She said confused.

'At first, yes, but then they realised that they all ended up washing dirty pots and picking endless strawberries.'

'Really?' She was now entranced. 'Do you know, I never really thought about it like that before.'

By this time Charles was forced to divide his time between picking bits of fluff from his jacket and imaginatively folding his napkin.

'They only use the North Coast as a staging point of course. Their real aim is Sub-Saharan Africa. It's something to do with being "valued" down there,' he added.

'Well, I suppose... the Trust will be trying to organise, the relevant organisations, and... help the...Europeans live in peace with the Africans.' She looked down.

'Well, that's excellent.'

Charles initiated their evacuation from the table at the earliest polite moment. The exit was not as easy as he had anticipated due to his unwitting wife being quite taken with the hairy heathen. Practically prying his wife away from the situation, expressing goodbye wishes through a forced smile, ushering her away as she tried to arrange future "get togethers" with their tormentor. Once they were well away, Derek leaned back in his chair in a manner that suggested relaxation after a job well done. He beamed at Susan. She smiled back.

'You're a bad man Mr Rye,' She said, wagging her finger like a school teacher.

'Why thank you my dear. If it's any consolation to you, it is a badness that took me a long time to acquire.'

'A man capable of learning. That is a rarity.'

'What can I say? Knowledge just seeps into me, like oil into rock. How about another round of drinks eh? I think we've earned it.'

'I thought it got a bit cruel toward the end,' Jennifer said, 'Especially the African charity bit.'

'I quite agree,' Susan said.

They all looked at Derek.

'Alright, alright, not my finest hour. Anyway, it's only cruel if the person realises that you're making fun of them. And if they don't realise, it serves them right for being so unobservant,' he folded his arms in defence.

'The rest was hilarious though,' Susan said to coax him back.

Susan looked over to Jennifer.

'Apart from Mr Rye's light relief, I should imagine it must be hard for you two youngsters, having to put up with a ship full of old fogies?' she said to Jennifer.

'It's not too bad; a bit like going to my grandparents' ruby wedding anniversary - except for a week.'

'Well, I don't know what you were wearing for your grandparents' anniversary, but I'll guarantee you've given a lot of the old codgers a new lease of life tonight. You look *gorgeous* Jennifer.'

'Thank you so much. I mean the dress wasn't my choice or anything; it was just sort of hanging up in my wardrobe.'

'It looks lovely.'

'That's the one thing I'll give this ship,' Derek said, 'They know how to dress people.'

'Felt a bit odd though. I was just thinking as I walked to the bar – how do they know my exact size? The thing is practically tailored to me.'

'Perhaps God is abusing his omnipresence?' Derek quipped.

Evan kicked him hard under the table.

'Arhh, mmmrph' Derek grunted.

Before they realised it, the four of them were the last passengers in the dining hall. They got the hint when the waiter removed the tablecloth and the cleaner at the other end of the room fired up a vacuum cleaner.

'Shall we move to the Auditorium?' Derek said airily.

They all pushed back their chairs and made their way to the theatre. After all the drinks consumed, the path that Evan, Jennifer and Susan followed was inventive, walking around tables which were not actually in the way. Derek, who had drunk more than all of them, walked as straight as an arrow.

They filed into the darkness of the Auditorium which was buzzing with the noise of anticipation. Weaving through the maze of occupied tables, they kept going until Susan spotted a free table at the back.

The compare walked to the microphone stand at the centre of the stage and clumsily lowered it to fit his diminutive stature. He realised that he was being bathed in a wholly inadequate light and so shot an acid look up at the lighting technician, who had dozed off. About a minute passed before the spotlight found its mark. He introduced the act of the evening and gaited off stage, as far as it is possible for a short man to gait.

There was a pause, followed by a hush and then... they came on stage. There were six of them, clean faced and bursting with energy, like children's television presenters on cocaine.

They started singing.

They started dancing.

Derek groaned and crawled under his chair.

After two hours the lights came back on to reveal a mixture of responses. Some people clapped vigorously, having clearly enjoyed the show. Others looked at each other with raised eyebrows of disapproval; however, the vast majority clapped politely after having been just about entertained for a couple of hours. They had learned nothing new and would wake up in the morning with a two hour gap in their memory of the previous evening.

Derek did not see any of this because he was curled up under his chair with his eyes shut and his fingers in his ears. The irony being that if he wasn't pretending to be a leafy green lettuce in the dark cool larder of a farmhouse (a technique he learned from his second marriage counsellor) he might have been able to pick out some potential friends amongst the crowd.

Once the auditorium was all but empty, Susan rubbed his shoulder and coaxed him out with a half finished, flat whisky and coke. He looked up at her with scared and helpless eyes, like a puppy in a cardboard box which has just come back from the rough manhandling of the local vet.

'It's O.K, it's over now,' she said soothingly, passing him the drink. He awkwardly unfurled an arm which was trapped under his girth, reached for the glass and drank it like a man fresh out of the desert.

'Jennifer and Evan went to the Outlook Lounge on the top deck. There's a jazz trio on for a bit. Do you want to come?'

He nodded gently, still dazed.

She offered him her hand. 'Come on now Mr Rye, time to get up.'

He took her hand lightly and then rose strong and straight.

'How was it?' he asked.

'Simply delightful.'

'Really?'

'No. Honestly, you *do* know how to make a spectacle of yourself.'

'Spectacle, what are you talking about?'

'Now don't play games, you *know* you spent the last two hours under your chair and no clever words will make me believe otherwise.'

'Yes, I know I've been under my chair, but that is the only decent and logical course of action to take when confronted with the unimaginative, nauseating and soulless entertainment put before us. It's everyone else who is acting strangely. I mean how they can just sit there smiling and clapping is beyond me. It's wrong, just plain wrong, they should all be carted off to the funny farm, the lot of them.'

'You're a difficult man to be associated with, difficult but fun.'

'I'll take that as a compliment. Do you know it's nice to be associated with someone, as you so affectionately put it; both emotionally and practically.'

'Practically?'

'Yes, usually after a Captain's Dinner Show, I get woken up from my leafy lettuce state by the bar staff a good while after everyone has left. I tell you, no matter how they come across, those Filipinos have a wicked sense of humour. For example, a month ago I was woken with the usual broom handle prod, except to my surprise and to the shock of the broom bearer, I was completely naked. It turned out to be an end of employment prank by a few of the barmen at the end of their service.'

'You mean the staff aren't dead?!'

'Far from it; they just come to Purgatory for a few months to work off their sins. Heaven only employs them because they're such an amiable bunch – most of the time. I think they've got a pool going back on Earth called "the funniest thing you can do to Derek at the Captain's Dinner Party". So, what I'm really trying to say, Susan, is thank you for being here tonight to save what dignity I have left.'

'Leafy lettuce?' she said playfully.

'Dear me, is that the time?! We should really be joining the others on the top deck.'

They found Jennifer and Evan in the Outlook Lounge. They were sitting at a table, watching the band playing. Jennifer looked relaxed and was smiling, tapping the beat on her glass, whereas Evan still looked tense and out of place in her company. They walked over and greeted them. The music was quiet, and the lounge sparsely populated.

'What took so long?' Jennifer asked.

'Apologies my dear,' Derek said, 'I had some difficulty in re-adjusting to my surroundings, but I'm fine now, thanks to the aid of this wonderful woman.'

'Don't forget the left-over whiskey,' Susan said.

'Yes, well, that always helps in most situations.' Derek seemed distant as he spoke, more interested in something over Jennifer's right shoulder. Interest quickly turned into perturbation. He scrunched his eyes up and made the noise of a potato trying to cry for the first time. The others saw his distress and wondered what had come over him. Susan put a hand on the back of his head which was now nestled, face down into the table.

'What's the matter?' Evan enquired with a firm voice laced with suspicion.

Derek said nothing. He remained motionless, except to raise a feeble shaking finger to the entrance of the lounge. Sure enough, the source of distress was quickly identified as Charles' wife. As she occupied the doorway, the light from the corridor streamed around her body making her appearance that little bit more disturbing. She scanned the room, struggling to adjust to the darkness of the lounge. They turned back to Derek, who was no longer there.

'Psst,' Came the rasping noise from under the table below where Derek had been sitting a few seconds before. 'Come on, what are you waiting for? Under the table!' he pleaded earnestly from his impossible position.

Charles' wife had spotted them by now and was winding her way toward the table.

'Quick, quick, before it gets here.'

Susan - in a unique show of social skills and multitasking - kicked Derek hard whilst standing to greet Charles' wife.

'There you all are!' Charles' wife enthused, 'I've been looking all over for you, and you've been hiding up here the whole time.' She quickly raided a spare chair from the neighbouring table and made herself at home.

'Where is Charles?' Susan asked politely.

'Oh, he's gone to bed, said something about a headache. I apologise on his behalf for him being so unsociable.'

She looked at them and then around at the lounge. 'Where is Derek? He doesn't seem to be the type for an early night.'

Susan thought quickly.

'He's just popped back to his cabin to fetch something.'

'Ah.'

What followed was a long silence in which the three of them exchanged quick glances and then stared at their drinks for a while. Any person with keen social awareness would have clocked this and realised that they were interrupting the conversation and were generally not wanted. Charles' wife was not such a person. Not even close.

'So, did everyone enjoy the show?' She persisted.

She heard three noises of elongated neutrality.

Having enjoyed the show immensely, she was surprised and disappointed by this response. It was the fourth noise, however, that surprised her the most. Surprised and confused her because it didn't seem to come from any of the three other people around the table.

'Well, I thought the musical about the three American servicemen and their turbulent yet rewarding relationship with three English roses was brilliant.'

The fourth noise occurred again, but a bit louder this time and the table shuddered.

'Did anyone hear that?' Charles' wife asked. Again, this was met with three noises of elongated neutrality.

'Yes.' Came the very matter of fact response from the phantom fourth person.

Charles' wife located the voice as coming from underneath the table. She pushed back her chair a little way, peered into the darkness and started to prod the lump thing curled up on the floor.

'Do you mind, that's my eye you happen to be prodding,' complained the Derek lump.

'Oh sorry.'

'Yes, sorry indeed. How would you like it if I came into your bedroom in the middle of the night and started prodding your eye just out of idle curiosity?'

'Derek? Is that you? Oh, it is, how very funny! You really are a card!'

'Yes, it's me,' he grumbled as he heaved himself back into his seat with an air of depression. 'Ta-dar,' he lethargically added with the matching hand gestures.

'My dear Derek, what on earth were you doing under there!'

The way that she said it, made Susan prickle.

'Hiding from you,' he said levelly. This made Charles' wife burst out into forced laughter and slap her thigh.

'Good show!' she exclaimed loudly. It was now clear that Derek could do no wrong in her eyes and that simply mocking the intrepid creature would not be enough to get rid of it.

Altogether more sly methods were required if they were going to regain their evening from the jaws of ruin.

'My round, is it?' Derek said brightly, looking at everyone.

'Right then, to the bar. Susan, would be so kind as to accompany me? They both got up and wandered over to the bar, leaving Jennifer and Evan with Charles' wife. After a brief and uncomfortable pause Jennifer stepped up and began a faltering description of the jazz trio which had been on earlier for the benefit of Charles' wife. This trailed off into another uncomfortable silence which was only interrupted by the return of Derek and Susan with a tray of drinks.

Jennifer helped herself to the one that looked the most alcoholic. Derek finished his drink quickly. Well, Derek always finished his drinks quickly, however this time he finished it faster than usual. He placed the empty glass down thoughtfully and then stretched out with a great yawn, like a bear about to settle for its winter hibernation.

'I think I'll call it a night,' he said. 'I've had a little too much to drink.' This was clearly not true, and Evan realised that Derek had said it in order to alert him to the fact that this was another of his elaborate ruses of which Evan would no doubt become a reluctant accomplice. Derek wished them a good night and walked out of the lounge.

Susan was more tactful, but not much more. She waited for at least a whole four minutes before draining her glass, complaining about a headache and then disappearing out the same way.

With just the youngsters left, Charles' wife felt a little uncomfortable and out of place. After a few minutes, she made her excuses, gathered up her shawl and exited.

'And then there were two,' Jennifer said spookily. Evan looked around and saw that apart from the barman who was busy buffing glasses, they were the only people left in the Outlook Lounge.

'I guess that's one of the drawbacks with being on a ship full of old people,' Evan said.

'I should probably go some time soon. I mean the sooner I get to sleep, the sooner I'll get a really bad hangover, and then the sooner I'll get over it,' Jennifer said with a tired smile.

'I wouldn't leave just yet. I've got a feeling that Derek and Susan will be back quite soon.'

Jennifer looked at him.

'You mean all that going to bed stuff was just a way of getting rid of what's-her-face!'

'When you know the beast, you know what it's capable of. I'll get you a glass of water; that usually helps with the hangover.'

'Thanks,' she said tired but sweetly.

Evan walked to the bar, gathering his racing thoughts as he did. As the barman was pouring the water, Evan saw Jennifer move from the table, walk past the bar and settle herself down in one of the sofas in the far corner of the lounge. She had slipped off her shoes and was curled up, resting her head on the arm rest, her red hair cascading freely.

He brought the water over to her and sat down on the opposite seat not quite knowing whether to disturb her or not. She opened her eyes, sensing his presence and took the glass from him.

'What are you doing all the way over there?' she asked softly, 'Come over here.'

Evan got up, a bit uncertain of himself and plonked himself down next to Jennifer, who had shifted a little to accommodate him.

'I just need to rest for a while, just wake me up when the others arrive.' Evan sat there feeling torn between happiness and fear: Happiness that he was so close to her, but also fearful that he might not come up to her expectations. Tiredness won through, however, and he drifted off to sleep where he sat.

Derek and Susan made their way up the flight of stairs, rounded into the corridor and breezed into the Outlook Lounge. They surveyed the area but could not see the others. Susan nudged Derek and pointed into the corner at the opposite end of the room. There, they saw Evan sat upright on the sofa, fast asleep with his head nodded forward. Jennifer was leaning up against him with her head nestled on his shoulder.

Heaven Dawns

The next day, the darkness that had enveloped them began to give way to the awesome light of Heaven. They stood at the port side railings on the Sun Deck and watched the light emanating from the shimmering membrane.

'It's beautiful,' Jennifer said, clasping Evan's arm.

Derek seemed detached as he gazed into the distance.

'You OK Derek? It's not like you to be stuck for words,' Evan said.

'No I'm fine,' he said dreamily, 'it's just…'

'Just what?'

'Oh, take no notice boy. I'm probably just going soft in my old age.'

The four of them stood in silence as they watched the light getting brighter by the second and listening to the soft rhythmical sound of the hull against the ether. As they got closer, Evan noticed movement on the horizon; small blips of white, that appeared and then disappeared as quickly as they had come. After a while, the blips could be distinguished as white blades that were moving in an arc above the horizon.

'What are those Derek?' he asked.

'Rather nice aren't they,' Derek replied, 'Well, I think so.'

'What is Heaven doing with wind turbines? I mean, doesn't everything run on the glory of God?'

'A Watt of glory to boil a kettle; and don't switch on your electric heater when God's busy, because it might divert too much of his power,' Derek said sarcastically.

'Oh, stop being so hard on him,' Susan said affectionately.

'He brings it on himself you know,' Derek said, 'Seriously, I haven't the first idea why they're there. All I know is that they built the first one about three years ago and they've been adding more and more since.'

They passed through the membrane and into the harbour. The entrance was about four hundred metres wide, and each end was adorned with two huge ornate statutes of angels; each had two swords crossed against their chests. The stone angels stood on the sea wall hewn from glistening marble.

On top of the seawall, there was a walkway with a parapet structure on the seaward side. It looked more decorative than defensive, like the parapet of a French château. Once inside the seawalls, the ether turned into a calm blue body of water, stretching out in front of them for about a mile; flanked each side by the marble seawall as it joined back to the shore.

There were over a hundred turbines standing inside the harbour walls, slowly swishing like majestic, white giants. Small recreational boats weaved in and around their bases but looked tiny compared to the girth of Purgatory, making Evan wonder whether the ship would be able to get through the maze of white pillars.

An escort of two angels swooped into view, taking their positions just off the bow of the ship. They were dressed in white cloth, embellished with formal designs. The lacklustre way that they beat their wings suggested that this was routine, rather than a spontaneous welcome party. The ship docked with the effortless ease with which it had arrived at the jetty on Earth and the engines cut out.

'Well, this is goodbye,' Derek said with rare emotion in his voice.

He turned to Evan.

'Evan, my boy, it has been a pleasure,' he said and thrust his hand forward in a strangely formal manner.

'Goodbye Derek,' he said, whilst taking his hand. 'I never would have imagined death could be so entertaining until I ran into you.'

'A fine compliment; a fine compliment,' Derek replied and then paused. 'I thought that such a moment might arise, so I took the liberty of gathering some farewell gifts, so bear with me.'

He fished around in his jacket pocket and produced a stained, slightly deformed beer mat; a half empty pepper dispenser; and miniature bottle of whiskey.

'To you Evan,' he started in a haughty voice, 'I give a beer mat, so that any future spillages in the afterlife may be mopped up without embarrassment.'

Jennifer laughed.

'To Jennifer,' he said twisting his body slightly, 'I give the pepper seller, so that you may forever have spice in your life.'

She took it from him with a look of contented confusion.

'And finally, to my dear Susan; our time together has been brief but wonderful, and to you I give this miniature whiskey to remind you of me.'

Susan thanked him with a kiss.

Evan, Jennifer and Susan dismounted Purgatory with the rest of the excited passengers and spilled out onto the harbour wall. To one side of the open-air dock, close to the hull there was a musical ensemble, which played an upbeat farewell tune with about thirty of the staff doggedly singing the unfamiliar English lyrics. There were also a couple of temporary registration booths set out in the large stone quad. After getting over the "we're in Heaven!" euphoria, the passengers formed two orderly queues. Jennifer and Susan went through with the rest whereas Evan was separated and told to wait to one side.

Once the dock was cleared of the new intake, a thickset man walked up to Evan.

'Evan Edwards?'

Evan nodded.

'I'm Tom, the domestic and maintenance manager. You've been assigned to me.'

Evan just looked at him.

'Grab your stuff, oh you haven't got any, well we can supply you with all you'll need. Follow me and I'll show you to your dormitory. Then we'll get a cup of tea and I'll fill you in on the basics.'

Working and Wondering in Paradise

The dormitory was basic. A small man was sat cross-legged on the bottom bed of the far bunk, studying parchments laid out in front of him. He stood up gingerly as they entered.

'Hi Dali, we've got a new boy in today. This is Evan,' Tom said.

Dali nodded politely. 'Pleased to meet you,' he said in a serene voice.

'Do you think you could show him around, until he gets settled in?' Tom said.

'Of course, my pleasure,' Dali smiled.

'The others are out at work, but you'll meet them all tonight. I'll put a brew on. Do you want one Dali?'

'Yes please, decaffeinated coffee.'

'Lots of brandy eh?!'

Dali laughed, 'Yes, lots of brandy - A Buddhist latte.'

Tom turned back to Evan, 'Right then, come into my office, it's just across the way.'

Evan followed him into a messy looking room. Yellowing posters adorned the chipped, plaster walls; a worn motorcycle leaned on its stand in the corner, with its front wheel missing and oily parts on the floor next to it. The desk was laden with piles of disorganised papers and used coffee mugs. One whole wall was taken up with shelving which groaned under the weight of assorted spare parts and other useful bits, which no maintenance man would dream of throwing away. He gestured for Evan to sit in the upright wooden chair opposite his own upright wooden chair, behind his desk. He put the kettle on and sat down.

'Welcome to Heaven.'

Evan realised that he was the first person to say this.

'You didn't expect to work when you got to paradise, but that's the way it has happened. It's really not so bad: the work is simple and I try to keep our team happy.'

Evan smiled weakly.

'O.K then. Firstly, do you have any experience in maintenance?'

Evan shook his head.

'Not to worry, you'll pick it up as you go along.' The kettle boiled. Tom rose and busied himself with the drinks. He left the room to ferry a cup of coffee back to Dali and then came back in sipping at his mug as he walked.

'Any questions?'

'How long do I have work for each day?'

'Keen to get stuck in, that's what I like to hear,' Tom said jovially. 'It's the regular eight-hour day, same as back on Earth and alternate weekends off. However, unlike Earth you don't actually get paid anything; but then again you are in Heaven so it sort of balances out.'

Evan looked despondent.

'I've got to go and check up on a few things,' Tom said, 'so I'll leave you to your own devices, but be back at the dorm by say about six o'clock for the daily debrief.'

Tom led the way out into the corridor and went off to make his rounds, leaving Evan next to the open doorway. Dali was sitting on the end of his bed drinking his coffee.

'Hello Evan. Please come and make yourself at home. This *is* your home after all. However, it is *my* home also, so I must insist that you take your shoes off and meditate at least five times a day.'

Jennifer was taken to a plush, white suite in a block all by herself. She idly turned the key in her hands, which read – room 2047.

2047, she thought, *how many rooms does this place have?!* She walked over to the French windows; fought with the heavy curtains; opened the glass door and stepped out onto the balcony. She knew that the harbour, beach and main facilities lay behind her, but looking out in the opposite direction, there seemed to be no end to the Spanish villa style blocks, which stretched out to as far as she could see. The buildings were quiet. She flopped onto the large, quilted bed, stared at the white ceiling and wondered how Evan was getting on.

Evan looked at Dali with an uncertain smile. Dali looked back with a staunch expression, and so Evan removed his shoes.

'Now, we will have mid-morning meditation. Sit down facing east please.'

Evan looked around, unable to find east.

Dali made a large expression of exasperation and pointed at Evan's shoes.

'East is the direction of your left shoe - always.'

Evan timidly sat down beside his left shoe.

Dali came and knelt beside him and fitted some small chimes to the end of his fingers.

Chime

'Now repeat the chant after me please.'

Chime

'Whyareyousogullibleahhhh.'

After repeating the chant a few times, Dali could no longer contain himself and toppled over sideways in a fit of soft laughter. At first Evan didn't understand but it soon sunk in. He felt suddenly angry and so reached over and grabbed the chimes from his fingers.

'Hey! You never take the bells from a Buddhist!' Dali said with grave feeling.

'Well as a guest in *my* home,' Evan said with glee, 'I insist that you refrain from using your bells when indoors.'

'But...' Dali protested weakly.

'Oh yes, and drink five cups of tea per day!'

Jennifer got herself a drink and walked along the deserted beach. 'Hicup this place is dull,' she said. She was trying to say, 'God this place is dull.' So was surprised and annoyed that she was now being censored by unknown forces. Just out of spiteful experimentation she shouted as loud as she could:

'Jesus Christ and the Virgin Mary what's wrong with this place!' Which came out as, '*hicup, hiccup* and the *hiccup, hiccup* what's wrong with this place!' She hurled her drink into the sea, snapped the straw in half and then kicked at the sand in exasperation.

Two men came scurrying out of a nearby shed. The first ran over to her; picked up the broken straw and hurried off in the direction of the bar; whilst the other man waded into the sea, dived a few times and eventually emerged triumphant with the glass in his hand. By the time the second man had made it back to shore, the first was back and handing Jennifer a new cocktail. She smiled a wry smile. Without delaying the fun, she lobbed her cocktail down into the sea, and once again the two men leapt into action. Content, she settled down into a recliner and let the midday sun wash over her.

She was woken from her doze by the sound of nearby chattering. She lazily opened an eye and saw a couple of the angels on the beach, lugging around pink exercise mats, with a man in a robe close by.

'Hey,' one of the angels said in a friendly voice, 'new, are you?'

She nodded.

'We're setting up for a Pilates class; you're welcome to join us.'

'Where is everyone else?' Jennifer asked frankly.

The angel frowned and then shrugged. 'It's not as popular as it used to be, but we carry on. Apart from Aristotle that is, he always joins us,' the angel said indicating the elderly man in the robe, who smiled weakly.

'I find that it helps the body to balance its four humours,' Aristotle said, 'thus freeing the mind to explore deeper meanings of life.'

The angel laughed and patted him on the shoulder.

'Don't be fooled by the dry old philosopher act; he's as limber as the Chinese state circus.'

After work, the next day, Evan met up with Jennifer.

'What do you want to do?' she asked casually.

'Maybe go for a wander along the seawall?'

'O.K,' she smiled.

They left the Sun Plaza and were halfway across the dock before she spoke.

'How was work?'

'I was on litter duty all day.'

'On the beach?'

'In the morning.'

Jennifer laughed, 'Good thing I wasn't there this morning.'

'Eh?' Evan said confused. Jennifer realised what she had said.

'Oh no, not because I'm avoiding you.'

They walked a bit further in silence. They had walked about half a mile when Jennifer stopped in her tracks. Evan broke from his daze and stopped too.

'Evan?' she said, 'Do you like me?'

Evan frowned. Possibly not the best reaction.

'Because I really like you,' she said.

Evan's heart did something irregular and for some reason he felt despondent.

'What's wrong?' she said with a frown 'Do you actually like me? Or are you just saying that?'

'I...I...It's complicated.'

'Fine,' She huffed and started to walk back to the shore.

Evan stood still. His mind divided between letting her leave and confiding in her. He saw his one chance of happiness walking away and made up his mind.

'Wait Jennifer.'

She turned around, 'Why?'

'Walk with me a little further...Please?'

They walked all the way to the base of one of the huge stone angels and sat down facing each other on the marble walkway.

'I like you,' he started, 'but I'm afraid.'

'Afraid of what?'

Evan breathed out heavily, wrestling with his mind to talk.

'Afraid that I won't come up to your expectations.'

'In what way?' she said interested.

'You're a beautiful, strong, intelligent woman, whereas I'm just me. I'm not manly in the normal way and I don't know much about stuff...'

'...I don't mind,' she said.

'You'll just get bored with me.'

'I think that you're a really nice guy, the kind of person I could see myself spending a lot of time with. And let's face it; we've got a lot of it to fill,' she said reaching over and rubbing his shoulder. Evan laughed and wiped his eyes.

'There is that.'

Evan woke up thanks to the pre-arranged prod administered by Dali. He groaned and rolled out of his bed and onto the hard, cold wooden floor. This was the only method that managed to shock him into any kind of useful consciousness at eight in the morning. Just as the team was trundling out to work, Tom called for Evan from his office.

'I've got a special job for you today; you're young, aren't you? And you're into whatever young people are into, right?'

'I suppose.'

'Good, because I want you to do some gardening.'

He followed Tom's directions. The small wood was well out of the way, about a mile from the beach and a respectful distance from any of the residential blocks. Nestled at the base of a couple of the larger trees, was a dilapidated caravan. It lay peacefully with a small vegetable garden cultivated in front of it, with crazy paving up the middle.

He got in amongst the vegetables and began to pull at the weeds. The caravan curtains twitched, and he saw a face behind the glass. There was a commotion in the caravan; the top half of the split horse box door was flung open in earnest.

'Get off my vegetable patch!' the man cried.

Evan stopped digging and looked at the long-haired man.

'Just doing my job,' he said raising his palms.

'Who sent you?' the man asked suspiciously, turning his head slightly.

'My manager.'

'Typical. Did he tell you to knock on my door and have "a nice chat" with me as well?!'

'No,' Evan answered plainly.

The man huffed and then deflated in posture.

'Suppose it's not your fault. It just gets to me that's all.'

'Who are you anyway?' Evan asked.

'Didn't they say? Well, I'm Jesus. Jesus who lives all by himself in a dilapidated caravan. What? I hear you say: Jesus, the Lamb of God, at the right hand of the Almighty lives in a caravan?! Yes, that's right. And he doesn't like to have visitors either, no matter how many potential "buddies" the council try to force on him.'

'Are you alright?' Evan said, genuinely concerned about the guy.

Jesus gave a dismissive hand gesture.

'You wouldn't understand,' he said as he closed the top half of his door.

Evan finished weeding Jesus' garden to the sound of tortured acoustic guitar.

After work, Evan looked at the scrap of paper that Dali had given him. He knew the time and place written on it but had long learnt not to trust his poor memory. Carrying on down the stone flagged corridor, he emerged out into the Sun Plaza, which was already thronging with people and the buzz of debate.

A man was standing on a soap box. His mouth was opening and closing, and sounds were coming from it, but it took a second or two to distinguish his words from the noises of the babbling crowd around him.

'Thank you, ladies and gentlemen, for coming out today to be involved in this week's democratic debate,' Aristotle called above the din, trying to get their attention focused on the debate rather than the exchange of the week's gossip.

Aristotle introduced the first speaker of the day, Phillip Watts, who mounted the small, upturned box and cleared his throat. The tight throng nearest to the speaker remained quiet and increased in attentiveness. The socialites at the rear simply acknowledged the speaker with a token silence and then carried on gossiping, using the speaker as a pleasant background to their activities. Aristotle produced a sand dial, turned it upside down and nodded at Mr Watts.

'May I first start by thanking the organisers of today's debate, without who's magnificent commitment to the democratic process; we would all surely be at a loss,' said Mr Watts.

Many of the spectators nodded and murmured in agreement.

'Over the last three years, the expansion of the wind power programme has gone from strength to strength. From its conception to the instalment of the first offshore turbines, to the one hundred and thirty eight turbines that we have in operation today, Heaven has seen more and more of its energy needs met by a clean, renewable and secure source. The data collated from the last twelve months has unequivocally shown that the turbines have been a sound investment and a resounding success. The building, running and maintaining of the turbines has contributed greatly to Heaven's micro-economy with hundreds of angels and residents involved in their construction. Any excess power generated is now being sold to Earth via our new two-thousand Mega Watt inter-dimensional inter-connector thus creating more revenue to spend on making Heaven even more blissful.'

'What like an extra Pilates class every week?' a resident heckled. Aristotle glared angrily at the heckler, pointing at his sand dial. Mr Watts shrugged it off with a laugh saying it was an issue for the events co-ordinators to decide and carried on.

'The scheme has been developed with the greatest sensitivity to the local environment and has been designed to minimise the visual impact on the residents of Heaven. Any negative environmental impacts have been offset with conservation schemes such as the new jellyfish cove, we have built to compensate for lost habitat. The turbines also ensure a security of supply of energy. Heaven is much less dependent on God's power which can vary greatly depending on what mood he is in.' Aristotle tapped his glass dial to show that there were only a few grains left. Aristotle thanked him for his speech and politely ushered him from the box.

'To remind everyone of this week's debate title once again,' Aristotle announced. '"Meeting Heaven's energy needs".' He stopped to clear his throat. 'Our next speech is from Mrs Janice Worthing who is the leader of the local pressure group – "No Turbines in Heaven".'

She got up and held the audience with a confident, well-practised gaze. 'Heaven does not need any more turbines. It has far too many as it is and the addition of any more would be a great mistake. Socially, they are an eyesore, both for the individual; and a blight on Heaven's natural seascape. I am sure that Mr Watts can place, sculpt and colour them in the most "sensitive" way, however he cannot make them disappear. They will always be spinning, exoskeleton contraptions that naturally catch the eye. When people come to live in Heaven they surely expect to be met with sandy white shores and crystal-clear blue waters. They do not expect to be forced to live beside these gigantic monsters which Mr Watts has constructed. They are an infringement of our civil liberties and our human rights. No one should have to live next to them for eternity.'

'Then there is the noise. One or two turbines would not be an issue, however with so many, the level of noise increases greatly. Turbines begin to beat in phase with each other thus creating larger disturbances, as the blades cut through the air. An expansion of the programme would exacerbate this problem. We are also concerned about the impact on the harbour's marine ecology. Although a cove has been constructed for displaced jellyfish, our research has shown that some of these creatures are in fact sedentary and would not naturally migrate away from the construction sites.'

'We would like to see the council explore other option other than wind as the method for supplying Heaven with its energy. The ether, for example, is an abundant potential source of energy. Such a tidal scheme would provide more reliable energy and would be equally as sustainable as wind.'

She stepped down from the soap box and Aristotle meticulously waited for the remaining few grains of sand to disappear before thanking Mrs Worthing for her speech. He then got back on his box.

'And now we throw the floor open for questions to be put to our two main speakers.' Evan held up his hand assertively. Aristotle saw this and nodded in his direction.

'Yes, I'd like to put a question to Mr Watts please.'

'Introduce yourself first please.'

'Evan Edwards.' Aristotle made a friendly gesture to indicate him to proceed. 'Mr Watts. What measures have you put in place to deal with the intermittency issue presented by a large wind energy programme?' Everyone looked at Evan as if he had just asked his question in Swahili, except Mr Watts who broke out into a minor sweat. Evan sensed that most of the congregation did not understand his meaning and so he clarified.

'What I mean is: How do you plan to supply Heaven with the energy it needs when the wind is not blowing? What dedicated back up generation have you put in place to allow for the vagaries of the wind?' An intense murmur spread throughout the crowd.

Mr Watts began to laugh heartily. 'I think the boy has missed his afternoon nap and got himself all worked up about nothing!' The crowd started to laugh as well, making Evan go red with fury.

Aristotle, being a stickler for formality waited for the crowd to die down and then asked Mr Watts to answer the question put to him.

'As has been the case since the wind programme began, we do have a traditional generator which is switched on when the wind doesn't blow.'

Evan felt frustrated. He had naively believed that bringing up a poignant point in a democratic debate would be enough to sway the vote. Once Aristotle had counted the black and white voting pebbles, he had announced that Heaven would continue with the expansion of the wind energy programme.

He told Dali the whole story but to Evan's disappointment, Dali was not surprised by the outcome.

'I had the same problem with Chairman Mao,' he comforted. 'You cannot give up after the first hurdle my friend, or the second or the tenth, otherwise you will achieve nothing.'

'Wait a minute, Chairman Mao? The deceased Chinese leader?'

'Yes.'

'And you're a Buddhist.'

'Yes.'

'And your name is Dali.'

'The Dalai Lama, well, one of them, yes,' Dali said.

'But I thought that Buddhists don't believe in God?'

'St Peter and I had a long and fruitful debate, and he came to the conclusion that I was the victim of geographical dislocation from the teachings of Christ, and that I could therefore enter Heaven as a cleaner.'

Immortally Binding Contract

Evan was scrubbing some flagstones when Tom tapped him on his shoulder.

'Hi Evan,' he said.

'Hi Tom,' Evan said without looking up from his rhythmical strokes, 'I know I'm a bit behind, but I'll definitely get to unblocking that toilet by the end of the day.'

'No, it's not about that. Look you'd better stop scrubbing and stand up a minute. I don't quite know how to say this,' Tom continued now that they were face to face, 'but the foreign affairs department of the council want to see you.'

Tom's eyes became dewy.

'What's wrong?' Evan asked.

'I just want you to know that you've been a good member of the team.' Tom said shaking Evan warmly by the hand. With that he turned and walked off back to his workshop.

Evan made his way to the council buildings, his mind running theoretical eventualities that fitted in with Tom's strange behaviour.

He was shown to the councillor's office as soon as he arrived.

'You wanted to see me?' Evan said flatly, surprised at his own forthrightness.

'Yes. Please have a seat,' the councillor cooed.

Evan sat and folded his arms but realised that he was still gripping a scrubbing brush. He placed the brush on the floor and tried to make the white lather all over his chest seem deliberate.

'As you are aware, you are in the services of Heaven, subject to an immortally binding contract,' the minister said, flicking his eyes from Evan's face, down to the drooping foam, then back to Evan's face.

Evan nodded sensing that something unpleasant was about to asked of him; something that only a contract with God would make him do.

'You have been selected to partake in our reconnaissance programme. A highly important task, that keeps us abreast of what's going on beneath the stairs.'

'I can assure you, there is nothing going on under the stairs because I have to go under them every morning to fetch the mops,' Evan protested.

'You miss understand. We're sending you to spy on Hell. I have some angels who are amending your sin resume as we speak.'

'But doesn't God know everything that goes on down there anyway? He is supposed to know everything isn't he?'

'Yes, he does. However, he is on holiday.'

'What? Where does God go on holiday?!'

'His creation - Earth. He likes to do jobs - postmen, nurses, teachers, that sort of thing. See how you all tick.'

'So, he'll be back in a few weeks then and you won't need me,' Evan said shortly.

'No, no, no "and on the seventh day he did rest" It is still the seventh day of creation and will be for quite some time. Now, report to archangel Francis for your full brief.'

He found Francis in the games room playing table-tennis with a Cherubim.

Ping, pong, ping 'Francis?' *ping pong.*

'Yep, that's me' *ping pong* Francis replied still engrossed in the game 'What can I do for you?' *ping pong.*

'I was told to report to you for a briefing.'

Francis caught the ball and placed it on the table.

'Evan Edwards?'

'That's right.'

'Come with me,' he said, as he gave the Cherub an apologetic look. They walked in silence to the area that the angels occupied and into a neat and tidy office with highly polished armour arranged in the corner.

'It's all basic. We get you into Hell by doctoring your sin resume, and then you just gather as much information as possible, to bring back to us. Clear?'

'I guess.'

'Good. Here is your notebook and pen.'

'What if something goes wrong?' Evan said, putting them in his pocket.

'I've got something to get you out of trouble if you should come across it,' Francis said, as he pulled open the desk draw and took two round white objects.

'These are penitence grenades. Just throw into a group of demons and they all fall to their knees in a praying position. It wears off after about an hour.'

Evan put the grenades in the pockets of his overalls.

'I'll take you to the porthole now.'

Getting into Hell

Evan groped his way through thick white smoke, opening his eyes very slightly to try and gauge where he was going. The smoke began to clear, and he heard booming voices and the quieter noise of people sobbing and hyper-ventilating. He was stood in a large cavern made of red rock. There were about ten booths strung out along the centre of the cavern, with barriers and turn styles linking them together.

The scene before Evan reminded him of the ticket booths at the entrance to an amusement park. Similar, except that instead of buying a ticket from overweight Americans, people were having their mortal sins recited to them by overweight demons. Instead of getting all excited about the prospect of being splashed with water by a friendly dolphin, many of them were crying. The only similarity, in fact, was the weight problem of the employees in the booths. Evan made a mental note to improve the quality of his comparisons and then joined one of the queues, forgetting his mental note.

The demon saw Evan walking toward him and fiddled with his bendy microphone that protruded from the tiny desk of his Perspex booth.
    'Name?'
    'Evan Edwards.'
    The demon typed at his computer. Once the information had come up on screen, the demon took a deep breath, billowed his chest and began to boom in a theatrical voice, 'Stand before me puny wretch as I recite to thee thy mortal sins that have caused thee to be cast down into the pits of eternal damnation: You

assassinated John. F. Kennedy; snatch live organs; and hold an aubergine to be the one true God.'

'That's me,' Evan said brightly in the sure knowledge he was innocent of all of these.

'In that case I'll give you this ticket – hang on, I've got one somewhere,' the demon said, as he twisted his obese mass inside the booth. 'Here we are, show this to the duty demon and he'll take you to your cave. With staff shortages, we put really evil people to productive use. I'll start you off in information retrieval as an assistant. Doesn't sound much, but it's close to the action.'

The duty demon grunted in annoyance when Evan showed him the ticket and snapped at one of his human employees to take Evan to his new quarters, as he went back to dealing with Hell's new arrivals.

The employee was young, jittery and introduced himself as Quinten. He apologetically guided Evan through the rest of the intake cavern, past the newly damned who were being shackled together. They went through a narrow gorge of rock and then emerged on to a wide platform. What Evan saw took his breath away. From this vantage point, he could see the whole of Hell laid out below him.

It was shaped like an enormous bowl made from red sandstone. Large fires, small fires and torches were ablaze across the entire, eerie expanse. The lights seemed moody and temporary, as if at any point they would decide that illuminating this horrible place was no longer appropriate and would extinguish themselves. He could see thousands of tiny shapes moving around the vast bowl, and he wondered whether anyone actually knew how many poor souls were down here. The most prominent feature of this vista was the Gothic palace opposite them. Its foundations were rooted on the lip of the bowl rock, but its structure jutted menacingly out into the centre of the pit as if to affirm its dark authority.

'Come on then,' Quinten said, 'you don't want to be late for eternity.'

They walked slowly, side by side, down and down the sloping pathway which led to the torture pits. The employee began a guided tour of Hell's main features.

'That is the palace, where the dark prince resides,' he said pointing across to the mass of black buttresses, arches and gargoyles which conspired together to make a palace.

'The buildings on the lip over there,' he said pointing to a large section of the bowl's lip which had roughhewn structures sticking out of it, but not as dominant or impressive as the palace, 'those are the dark angels' and demons' quarters.'

'And where are our quarters?' asked Evan.

'On the opposite lip...they don't really like to mix with us humans – hired hands for the job, you understand.'

As they traversed the outskirts of the torture area, the tour degenerated into apologetic statements such as: 'This is...um well no... let's move on.'

He was shown to his cave. It was decent as caves go. There was a soft bed to sleep on and a view of the pits.

Quinten briefed him on where and when he was to report for work and scurried off back to the duty demon's yoke.

Information Retrieval

Evan entered the interrogation room. There were three people: A man standing up in a white, nylon, splash-proof bodysuit; a woman sitting down in the corner with a pencil and note pad; and lastly, the man waiting to be interrogated, who was strapped down to what looked like an old dentist's chair.

Like a dentist's chair, it had various sharp looking implements laid neatly in a stainless-steel tray. All three looked up at him with varying expressions on their faces: The interrogator lifted a quizzical eyebrow, annoyed at the interruption; the notetaker rolled her eyes at the prospect of more work due to the added person in the room; whereas the man strapped to the chair beheld Evan as his potential saviour, his eyes almost popping out in pathetic anticipation of Evan producing a last-minute reprieve document.

'Can I help you?' the man in a bodysuit muffled through his surgical mask.

'I was instructed to report here for work. This is information retrieval, isn't it?'

'That is correct,' he said pulling at his mask to lower it. 'Information retrieval is where you are. I personally like to put the emphasis on retrieval rather than the information. Let me fill you in on what we're up to. This is our first client for today,' he said pointing to the recumbent man, who, realising that Evan was not his last-minute saviour, had lapsed back into a quiet feverish panic. 'A Mr Ivan Edwards,' he said consulting a laminated sheet of paper attached to a pink plastic clipboard.

Evan nearly fell over, when he heard that name: the man who had gone to Hell in his place.

'Let's start off with some easy questions,' the interrogator said, yanking a chair from the side, spinning it around, and sitting on it back-to-front, trying to look friendly and easy going.

'Where do you live?'

Ivan blinked, thought for a long time and then answered in an almost inaudible voice.

'Slough.'

'Where in Slough?' he asked with sickly amiability.

Ivan's furrowed his eyebrows in confusion. After another long pause he plucked up some courage, 'Why?'

'Come, come, it's not a trick question, it's just for the files, so we can put people from the same town in the same cages – we're nice like that.'

'23 Alexander Avenue,' Ivan said weakly.

He went on to extrapolate other basic information about Ivan's friends, family, neighbours and work colleagues. Once finished, he looked over to the notetaker, who nodded firmly back at him, got up and scurried out of the room. The interrogator leaned back in his back-to-front chair, patted the side of his suit, produced a cigarette packet and lit a cigarette.

'Is that it?' Ivan asked, now more coherent, bordering on bright. He still had not recognised Evan.

'Nope,' the interrogator beamed with satisfaction. He stretched out his arm, as if offering Ivan a cigarette from his packet. Ivan looked at him and then wriggled his bound body as if to demonstrate that he was physically unable to accept this kind offer. The interrogator smiled and then, unable to contain himself any longer, threw his head back in raucous laughter, making Evan's blood chill.

The notetaker re-appeared and handed the interrogator some more laminated pieces of paper. He took some time to pore over them and once finished, placed them down on the table, except one and leaned in close.

'Let's start with your boss – Alex,' he sneered.

'What? I thought all that stuff was just for the files?'

'A little white lie I'm afraid, but necessary to facilitate the process. What are Alex's weaknesses?'

'What is this? Why do you want to know?'

'Just answer the question please.'

'Wait. You're going to use whatever I say against people who are still alive!'

The interrogator clapped slowly and deliberately.

'How did you think we know how to tempt people on Earth more effectively? My friend, morals have no meaning in this place. My advice to you is to abandon your Earthly values; they are of no use to you. I too was once in your position; a new arrival being interrogated and I too wanted to defend my friends and family. But then I realised that the machine was too large for one man to bring down. Telling me everything is just a natural progression, a burden lifted. How do you think I got to be where I am today?'

'By being sick?'

'No. By embracing the culture. And, If you co-operate, I might be inclined to put a good word in for you and who knows, you could escape Hell proper and become a part of the team. What do you say?'

'No.'

'Fine. If you won't answer questions about other people, maybe you will answer questions about yourself.'

'Never.'

'We'll see about that,' he said as he picked up a long tool with lots of curvy blades. 'Next question: What is your greatest phobia?'

'I'm not going to tell you that! I'm not stupid!'

'Tell me or I'll cut your eyes out.'

Ivan remained silent. The interrogator lost his patience and started in with the blade.

'Spiders!' Ivan squeaked, then broke down into sobs.

'Good.'

He swivelled his body around to face Evan who was still lurking, mortified, in the corner.

'Go down to the stores and get me a spider please. I'll just fill in a request form.'

He filled in a small chit and passed it to Evan. 'It's on the bottom level, second left after the armoury.'

Evan took it warily, now aware that he would now, adding insult to injury, be involved in the torture of Ivan.

Evan found his way back to the interrogation room and handed the interrogator a small box. He took it with glee and popped the lid to gaze at his new torture aid.

'What,' he said with iciness, 'is this?'

'Spider...It's all they had,' Evan added quickly.

'It's a daddy–long-legs,' the interrogator said, emphasising each word with disdain. Ivan's eyes widened and his jaw dropped in fear. He began to panic and writhe against his bonds.

The interrogator smiled and tipped the spindly creature out onto his palm.

'Excellent. Shall we begin?'

Ivan started screaming in the most horrible way.

'Once again I will ask you. What are your boss's weaknesses?'

Ivan just sobbed.

'You leave me no option but to set the spider on you.' He carefully guided the spindly creature onto his face. Ivan had degenerated into a fear-induced trance. The spider, of course, had no idea of what was going and so decided to migrate to somewhere warm and dark – Ivan's left nostril.

The interrogator rolled his eyes at the prospect of having "one of those days".

Ivan came too and started to snivel. The spider emerged from its cave-nose and peaked up at Ivan.

'Get it off! Arrgh! I'll tell you anything! Just get it off!'

'Alex's weaknesses?'

'Jane! She's one of the new employees at the office! He keeps talking about her when we're on the golf course! I think he's probably considering cheating on his wife!'

The interrogator removed the daddy-long-legs.

'Run that down to the temptation department please,' he said to the notetaker.

More questions were asked, and Ivan answered, under threat of the spider. Evan took Ivan back to his cage once his interrogation was over. Ivan was too preoccupied to recognise Evan, as he was returned to an eternity of suffering. Evan promised to himself that he would find a way of getting him out of this place.

The Brotherhood of the Soul Releasers

It was a troubling day working at information retrieval. He had assisted in processing three clients, making Evan wonder whether Heaven would allow him back in once his task was over. He wandered back to his room, past the wails and begging of the caged people in the torture pits. Once in his cave, he got out his notebook and pencil, and began to write down all he had seen during the day.

Quinten, the human employee who had given Evan a guided tour, was lingering outside Evan's cave.

'Hi Evan.'

'What do you want Quinten?'

'I thought you might want to come down into the bowl for the evening.'

'Why would I want to do that? It full of people being tortured.'

'Only during the day.'

They made their way from the workers accommodation down a craggy path, to the outskirts of the torture pits. Many of the flaming torches had been extinguished for the night and the cages were quieter. The path led out onto the Ongoing Productive Torture area, about halfway between the entrance booths to Hell and the dark palace. The damned were at rest for the most part. Many were asleep on the floor of their cages, huddled up against each other for comfort. Unlike those in Mind Soul Deterioration, these people were still very much human in spirit. A young woman sobbed quietly in the arms of an older woman who was rocking her slowly, like a child, trying to console her with soothing words. The older woman looked up at Evan in the semi-darkness with large black eyes. Her eyes were not angry or pleading, they were completely neutral, as if they were trying to make Evan look into them and reflect on his own soul. He stood still and looked but then looked away.

They took a wide sandy path that curved around the Ongoing Productive Torture area until they came to a well-lit street made from red sandstone bricks. Torches lined each side, planted into wooden brackets; a bright, changeable light coming from the oily rags that had been wrapped to the ends of the wooden poles and ignited. It was lined on either side with grimy drinking establishments and other buildings that had their windows blocked up.

Quinten led the way into the Human's Hovel. The Hovel consisted of a large open plan space with a long bar along the back wall, and an area on the left where there were private drinking booths. The large room was thronging with men and women, drinking and relaxing after a long day's torturing, implement sharpening, fire tending and other tasks that the humans were made to undertake in Hell. Quinten led the way to the bar, pushing a channel through the crowd.

The barman was a ghastly sight. Scars criss-crossed his pale face; his left eye was missing leaving shrivelled skin that grew back into the open socket. His good eye had a piercing and analysing force to its stare.

'Two beers please,' Quinten said to the barman in a subservient manner.

'Who's the new boy then?' the barman asked.

'This is Evan and he's alright,' Quinten said clasping Evan around the shoulder. Quinten gave the barman a small surreptitious nod of his head.

'We will see,' the barman said flicking his eye to Quinten.

They took their warm, sediment filled drinks and pushed their way through to the maze of booths. Quinten scouted around, poking his scrawny neck around corners and over partitions, sporadically turning to Evan and shaking his head. He eventually found a booth with a group of people that he was looking for. The four people sat in the small booth, all wearing worn trousers and torn shirts.

'Hey guys,' Quinten said as he squeezed through the narrow entrance, 'this is Evan.' The workers looked up with keen eyes and greeted him warmly.

'Take a seat. Shift up Noel, let the new boy sit down.'

'Where have they got you working Evan?' Noel asked

'Information retrieval,' he answered, whilst squeezing onto the tiny bench.

'Sadistic lot if you ask me.'

'They seem to take a lot of pride in their work,' Evan said.

'And do you?'

'Not really no; I feel sorry for the people being interrogated; having to betray their friends and family back on Earth.'

'How did you get to be an employee? If you don't mind me asking.'

'Aubergine worship.'

'Sorry?'

'Aubergine worship,' he repeated. The workers gasped, giving each other quick looks to see if the others had registered what Evan had said. One of the workers left his drink, slid of his bench without a word and went out of the booth in the direction of the bar, with a stony expression.

One of the workers turned to Quinten. 'What do you think Quin?'

'I think he's one of us,' Quinten replied.

The worker then looked at Evan across the stained, wooden pub table. 'I think that we should introduce you to some people Evan. How would you feel about that?'

'Sure, I'll meet some people.'

The worker who had left hurriedly for the bar returned to the tiny booth and gave Quentin a quick nod.

'Come on then Evan, time to go. Follow me.' Quinten said as he shifted past his peers and out of the booth. The scar faced barman was no longer serving drinks but had been replaced by another worker. Quinten lifted the bar top flap and held it up for Evan, before yanking open the double doors to the pub cellar. They went down the steps and into the dimly lit room. Wooden beer caskets lined each side of the cellar, three high, with a walkway up the middle. The scarred barman stood under the light of flaming torch at the far end. Quinten indicated that Evan should walk down the path. He went back up the steps, closed the double doors and left Evan alone with the barman.

'Do you know who we are?' the barman asked once Evan had walked up to him.

'No,' Evan answered.

'We are The Brotherhood of the Soul Releasers. Our purpose is to find and destroy the counterpart jellyfish of the damned that are in great suffering,' the barman stated, 'Do you wish to join us?'

'Yes.'

'Very good, but before you can be initiated, you must first go out into the ether to find and bring back your counterpart jellyfish. Quinten will show you to our boat.'

Evan emerged back up to the bar where Quinten was waiting for him. They pushed their way back through the crowd, toward the exit of the Human's Hovel, then out onto the sandstone street.

A group of demons were roaming around, their topless red skin sweating and glistening in the torch light. One belched loudly.

Quinten briefed Evan as they made their way back through the Ongoing Productive Torture area; past the workers quarters; through the Mind Soul Deteriorates, always hugging the curve of the bowl as they travelled. The night sky came into visibility as the cavernous roof of Hell gave way to the open air. They clambered over the jagged rocks, the cool night breeze coming off the sea and whipping over the ridge. They picked their way down the other side and eventually got down to the coarse sand beach. The boat was hidden in a small, eroded seam of the cliff that flanked the beach. They had to wade into the icy sea and get around a tight headland before getting to its secret location.

'Now remember,' Quinten said up to his waist in water and shivering, 'Just get the attention of a herder and they should do the rest.'

Evan pulled himself out of the freezing sea and into the rowboat.

'And make sure you're back by tomorrow morning, or else the duty demon will be on your case. So, if you are late, you'd better think of a convincing excuse that doesn't involve mentioning The Brotherhood.'

'Got it,' Evan said as he gained control of the oars and used one to push off from the cliff. The body of water was only a few hundred meters wide, and he had soon rowed through the dimensional membrane, and once again, found himself alone and surrounded by the eerie silence of the black inter-dimensional ether.

It was about twenty minutes before he came across a jellyfish, swimming alone through the ether. Evan drew up alongside it, reached over the side of the boat and lifted it onboard. This wasn't his counterpart jellyfish but was a way of getting the attention of one of the herders. Quentin had said that the herders are all finely a tuned to the welfare of each one of their flock and would immediately come to the aid of any jellyfish in distress. It was because of this that Evan now found himself pulling at its tentacles and prodding its nerve stem.

Soon enough a herder came into sight, travelling swiftly toward the boat on top of his dolphin steed. Evan soon recognised the herder as Ezekiel - the angel that had given him a lift back to Purgatory after he had fallen off the ship.

'Could you stop pulling the tentacles of that jellyfish please?' Ezekiel requested, not recognising Evan.

'Sorry. Hi Ezekiel, how are you?'

Ezekiel looked shocked at the mention of his name, but then his grey, dower eyes lit up with recognition.

'Evan! How are you? Would you like another chat?'

'Maybe later. I've got to ask you for another favour Ezekiel.'

'You haven't fallen off Purgatory again, have you?'

'No. I've got to find my counterpart jellyfish. Can you help?'

'Sounds like Brotherhood business to me.'

'Yes, it is. I'm being initiated.'

'Very well, I shall return within the hour with your jellyfish, and then we will have a good long chat.' Ezekiel's dolphin clicked and winced at his master's proposition.

'I'll be all ears.'

Ezekiel pulled around the reigns, dug in his heels and shot off back into the black ether.

Evan sat in his little boat and waited for the return of the herder. Once again he lapsed into thought. He reminisced about the last week he had spent in the afterlife dimensions: The strange escapades on Purgatory with Derek - his abnormal friend.

Meeting Jennifer - the person who kept him sane as he bounced around from one strange dimension to another. The thought of her would get him through this information gathering mission and back to Heaven. Even if he was a just a cleaner, he would be with her and that would be all that mattered. Then there was Heaven itself, a close-knit community of residents from throughout history under the friendly care of the angels. He hadn't thought much of paradise in the days he had been there, but now that he was in Hell, he had something to measure it against. Compared to the indifferent red rock, the demons, the constant pain of the damned and filthy conditions; Heaven really was a paradise worth living in for eternity.

Ezekiel re-appeared and came alongside the boat with a flourish.
    'Here is your counterpart jellyfish.' Ezekiel said handing it to Evan.
    'Thanks,' he replied, carefully cupping the translucent, slippery body and placing it on the deck of the boat.'
    'Sooo...' Ezekiel said.

Once the dolphin had called time on Ezekiel, Evan said farewell and rowed back toward the dimensional membrane with his counterpart jellyfish looking very pathetic and still at the bottom of the boat. He popped through the shimmering membrane and headed toward the eroded fissure in the cliff, where the boat was to be hidden. Once securely tethered, he waded through the icy shallows of the sea, back to the beach. Stuffing the jellyfish into the pocket of his overalls, he made his way back over the jagged rock; into the bowl, past the torture pits and finally back to the sandstone street lined with the pleasure houses of Hell.

It was later in the evening and so the street was livelier. A fight had broken out between a group of humans and a similar number of demons. They took ill aimed swings at one another and fell on their adversaries, pawing wildly at their faces. A demon who had detached himself from the medley shouted, "human scum, you should all be in the cages". A worker pinned to the ground by two demons shouted back "Red bellied bastards, did your mother sleep with a tomato!" before being pummelled in the face. Evan gave the whole scene a wide berth and slipped into the Human's Hovel. He pushed his way through the crowd, mindful to protect the side that housed his jellyfish. The barman saw him coming, said something to the worker next to him, and went to open the large double doors to the cellar.

'Welcome back,' the barman said as the two of them descended the cellar stairs, 'any trouble?'

'No.'

'Good.'

The barman went to the back of the cellar and stood facing Evan.

'Your jellyfish please Evan.'

He handed it over.

'Now that The Brotherhood has your counterpart jellyfish, you can begin initiation. If you tell anyone of the secrets we will divulge to you, we will terminate your jellyfish and therefore terminate you. Understand?'

'Yes.'

'Good.'

The barman turned to one of the beer caskets and lifted it open on a secret hinge. The whole top of the wooden barrel lifted away from the main body, at the far side. Inside the barrel were hundreds of jellyfish immersed in water. The barman eased

Evan's jellyfish into the open barrel and then slammed shut the lid.

'So now you know where we keep the jellyfish. Many of Hell's inhabitants are accounted for in our jellyfish tanks.'

'Why do you store them?'

'Patience.'

Evan left the cellar, went back out into the unruly street and picked his way back to his quarters. It had been a confusing day and all he wanted to do was get some sleep and hopefully wake up with a better perspective on things.

Satan's Personal Assistant

The next morning Evan was woken by the duty demon.

'Your presence has been requested by the dark prince. Report to the entrance chamber of the palace.'

Evan nodded, unsure of what was happening.

Evan walked into a large entrance cavern. Satan was already there. Evan lingered beside a small stool.

'SIT,' Satan boomed. He was standing with his back to Evan, perfectly still. Satan then turned around to face him, linking his hands behind his back.

'You want to be my personal assistant, do you?' he said, but in a smaller voice.

'I was told that...' Evan started.

Satan raised his red palm and then placed himself in an aggressive looking chair which had been fitted with sharp points and mammal skulls. He shifted uncomfortably in it, crossed his legs and began tapping his thigh.

'What experience do you have?' Satan asked.

Evan thought back over his idle life and realised that he had never really held a position of responsibility.

'None really.'

'Come, come, modesty, it says on your file that you worked at Enron as a personal assistant for three years. What about hobbies?'

'Snatching organs from living people,' Evan said, partially remembering his sin resume.

'Not that. Everybody has their guilty pleasures. I'm talking about your aubergines.'

'My aubergines?'

'Yes, you like to grow and idolise aubergines,' Satan said.

'Yes, that's right.'

'Interesting,' Satan murmured to himself, 'How do you grow your aubergines? Your horticultural techniques must be exquisite to produce a specimen fit for worship.'

Evan scratched his head. 'They have to be grown in a shoe - brown leather is essential.' He glanced at one of the skulls that Satan was idly caressing. 'Then the shoe is filled with compost derived from the rotted corpses of small mammals.' He wasn't sure whether Satan was buying it. A sweat broke out all over his body at the possible consequences of making fun of the dark prince, but it was too late to back out. 'Finally, water them every day with a fluid mixture of one part blood to three parts sweat.'

'Really?' Satan gasped in intrigue. 'Truly a master. Interview over.'

'When will I hear?' Evan blurted, his subconscious trying to inject some normality into the situation, before the rest of his mind packed its bags at the metaphorical circus.

'The job is yours,' Satan said.

Evan dithered as to whether to shake hands with Satan but decided not to – a bit too symbolic for his liking.

The next day Evan turned up at Satan's palace. He walked into the entrance cavern - the one which had been used as an interview room – stood and waited. No longer was the aggressive looking chair or Evan's small stool. There was subtle interplay of soft oranges, yellows, reds on the sloping, uneven walls.

'In here,' came a sad voice from his left. He swivelled his body and peered into a recess that led into another chamber. The inner cavern was smaller and more intimate than the first. A large fireplace was embedded into the rock of the far wall with much wood ablaze within. The spiky throne containing Satan faced the fireplace at a forty-five-degree angle and was mirrored by a smaller one. Satan did not look at him, just gestured nonchalantly for Evan to sit down on the spare chair. As soon as he planted himself down Evan realised that he was trapped in a silence in which Satan seemed to be lost in his own thoughts. He was caressing one of the armrest skulls to the point that it shone bone white. He would frown and breathe loudly through his nose as if his current line of thought had not blossomed to fruition.

Evan sat opposite, not quite knowing where to look or what to do but was nonetheless observing through the corner of his eyes. Satan continued his slow, mentally anguishing march towards epiphany, and every time he seemed to dry up, Evan would think that the silence would end, but it wouldn't. Satan would retrace his mental steps to the point where he had taken a wrong turn, and pick up a new thread of reasoning, nodded slowly, and then continue. Eventually Evan could no longer stand the silence and let out a small cough.

'Mrmm, what?' Satan said, awakening from his thoughts. 'Oh yes, thank you – um...'

'Evan.'

'Yes, Evan, that'll be all for today.'

'But I haven't done anything yet.'

'Haven't you?' Satan said looking up. 'Right then, I've an assignment for you. I want you to go and ask a sample of the damned to fill in a short questionnaire about the standards of service provision.'

'Service provision?'

'Are they getting enough food and drink every day; are the fires too hot; are the torturers being too rough on them etc.'

'But this is Hell, isn't it?'

'What?' The way that he said it tugged at something deep inside Evan. It was like Satan was an innocent child overhearing a conversation about how Father Christmas doesn't exist and that it's just Uncle Joe dressed up. He was flooded by a tide of empathy due to the realisation that Satan was not completely evil.

'Well, isn't Hell supposed to be a bad place to be?' he added softly.

'I know that,' Satan replied in a short, aggressive manner, 'The "eternal gnashing of teeth". It's just…I don't know,' he said, as he dropped his tormented head into the comfort of his hands.

All through his life Evan had contributed absolutely nothing to the advancement of humankind. Now, however, he had the chance to do something really worthwhile. Evan realised that this situation was perilously delicate. If one of the dark angels got to know of this, they would surely see their chance to grab power. Evan knew he had to hide Satan's good nature; maintain the tentative illusion that he was as evil as Hell itself.

'Why don't we amend this questionnaire for starters?' Evan said in a sympathetic voice.

'O.K,' Satan replied with watery eyes.

Evan left the dark palace with a spring of purpose in his step. He emerged from the entrance cavern, stood on the cliff edge and took in a deep breath. After violently spluttering the sulphurous air from his lungs, he composed himself and began the long trudge down the narrow, craggy pathway to the torture pits.

He made his way to the first group of the damned, who huddled in the centre of their primitive cage. The demons were leaning back on chairs, smoking cigarettes and playing cards. He caught the eye of one of them and asked if he could have a chat with the damned.

'Knock yourself out mate,' came the lethargic response, 'They're not due another jab for a while; and the tar's still heating.'

He swivelled to face the cage and its wretched contents. There must have been about twelve men, some old, some young, but all with gaunt faces and tattered loin cloths. They all bore looks of shock and bemusement, as if anything not connected to being brutally tortured was alien.

'Would you mind giving some of your time to fill out a questionnaire?' Evan said to the nearest man who was holding onto the bars with both hands and shaking violently.

'Murmef,' he dribbled. Evan took this to be a yes.

'Do you have any phobias of which the current administration is unaware of?'

'Ffffurrd,' the man dribbled some more.

'How could we possibly make things worse for you?'

'You won't get much sense out of this lot I'm afraid,' the cards playing demon piped up. 'They're MSD.'

'MSD?'

'"Mind Soul Deterioration". Begins after about a hundred years but varies from person to person. We still torture them, but they can't feel a thing anymore. I guess it's part of the deal – you do wrong on Earth, you get punished for eternity. After we've slapped a bit of hot tar over them, we'll just wheel them back down to the cellar with the rest of the MSDs. If I were you, I'd try further down, nearer to the centre of the pits. That's where the OPT damned are kept, "Ongoing Productive Torture".'

Satan's palace was the only prominent landmark that enabled Evan to know in what direction he was travelling. It sat on the lip of the bowl and dwarfed the surrounding structures. Rising and jutting out into the air above the torture pits. The further toward the centre Evan got, the denser the activities became. The people in the cages began to be more active and vocal, getting up when he walked past, begging for water, begging for help. Evan would stop, get out his questionnaire, but when he looked into their pleading eyes, he hadn't the heart to go through with it. He carried on his way, his heart sinking as he was engulfed more and more by the horrific scenes around him. His eyes began to get bleary; his body felt weak causing him to tremble as he walked. Above all though, he felt ashamed. He slumped to the floor, clutching at the dusty red earth as he sobbed and pleaded to be lifted from this place.

The Secret Vegetable Garden

Evan was once again sitting opposite Satan at forty-five-degrees in front of the blazing fire. Once again, Satan was deep in thought, looking vacant, occasionally changing to pensive. Evan had resigned himself to a long morning of keeping him in silent company, when Satan unexpectedly flicked his head up assertively.

'Can you keep a secret?'

'Of course,' Evan replied, resisting the urge to take out his notebook.

'I've never told anyone about this before,' he frowned at the floor and sighed deeply.

'I, I...have a vegetable garden,' he uttered, and then started to shudder and sob. Evan patted his large, red, hunched shoulders.

'It all started a couple of years ago,' Satan confided. Evan got up, put a few more logs on the fire and then settled back down.

'I knew it was wrong, even back then, but I was driven to it, do you understand? There was a time when I was the prince of darkness, the true prince of darkness. The years after the great defection from Heaven were difficult but we were united, and they all looked to me to keep the new way straight and true.' Satan seemed to transport himself into the distant past, his eyes glazing over, with the flames of the fire reflecting on his dark pupils.

'Go on,' Evan coaxed.

'Things began to stabilise out of the chaos. The dark angels were united in their common purpose – to create an antidote to Heaven. We built it - carved it from the very rock. I sat up high in the palace where we are now. I and I alone presided over this new domain, this new dimension, this new dream. I was feared and respected by all the minions of Hell. But then...'

'What?' Evan asked intrigued.

'I began to have thoughts.' He stopped speaking as if he had reached a more delicate aspect of his story.

'What kind of thoughts?'

'Intrusive thoughts.'

'What about?'

'I could control them at first and had to stop myself from acting on them. As time drew on, they began to get worse and worse. I began to get more urges, strong urges, to do...horticulture. The feel of the damp, crumbly soil on my fingers; the satisfaction of watching a small life grow from a seed into something leafy and beautiful; the joy of benign creation. Oh no, I'm sick, rotten to the core! I'm sorry for sharing my burden with you, but I had to tell somebody!'

'Why me?' Evan asked.

'The aubergines of course; I thought you could help me with my garden of shame. These last two years, my crops have been terrible, so I knew that I needed outside help. Once I read your sin resume, I knew you were the one to help me.'

Satan led the way further into his dark palace.

'I'm virtually kept prisoner in my own palace. None of the dark angels take me seriously anymore; they just encourage me to retreat deeper and deeper; so that is what I have done.'

He paused next a statue of a gargoyle and pulled its head to one side. This caused the rock wall to part, to reveal a secret passageway. Satan led the way inside.

'It has its advantages of course. I can get up to whatever I want to without any interference. And as I have proven; a mind left to wander free with no restrictions can lead to some very perverse things.'

'Horticulture.'

'Yes, but please stop saying that word - It upsets me.'

'Sorry.'

They reached the end of the long low, roughly hewn corridor and entered a small dark cave at the end. Evan could already smell a putrid aroma emanating from it and raised his hand to his face.

'Let me just light a lamp.' Satan said to himself and started bumbling around trying to make some light. Eventually Evan heard the strike of a match, and the cave was illuminated in a guttering light. There were two piles on the floor – one of old shoes, the other of dead animals.

'The shoes were easy to get, the mammals were a little harder, and I haven't been able to get hold of any sweat or blood yet. What do you think?' Satan turned to Evan with bated breath. Evan stared back in frozen panic.

'What's wrong? It's your secret formula so don't look at me like that. I am out on a limb you know.'

Memories of the interview came flooding back.

'Ohhh,' he relaxed, 'the formula. There is the quite large question of sunlight though.'

'Sun what? Oh yes, I remember the yellow stuff which comes from that dreadful star thing. What of it.'

'You don't have any down here. They need it to grow,' Evan clarified.

Satan looked dejected and slumped to the floor.

'It seems that I am destined to live a life unfulfilled here for eternity,' he said.

'Never mind, I'm sure there are other hobbies you could take up. What about pottery? There must be some clay around here somewhere.'

Circle of Evil

Later that day Satan took his token position at the head of the huge table. Evan stood at his side trying to look like he was supposed to be there. The rest of the dark angels sat at regular intervals along each side.

Archangel Argon arrived deliberately late and swished in with a grim, stony expression. All the angels sat up a little straighter. Argon sat down at the other end of the table, opposite the odd pair.

'Let us begin with last week's "circle of evil" agenda.'

He shuffled a loose stack of papers and looked up with a smug expression.

'The circle discussed the concluding points of operation "Homeland".'

He spread his hands on the table.

'We are ready! My inside man assures me that everything is set and all we need to do is wait for the right conditions. Once the inter-dimensional ether lays calm, Heaven will be ours!'

Evan went white and felt sick. The wind programme was Heaven's weakness. He thought of Jennifer.

The dark angels were clapping vigorously when he surfaced from thought. He looked over to Satan who was looking at his fingernails, seemingly not at all bothered about the imminent invasion of Heaven.

'Soon, Purgatory will pass our shores for the week, and we can assemble the invasion fleet at the beach head.'

Evan glared at Satan, pinching him hard to try and stir him into some sort of action. Satan winced, looked annoyed and mouthed "what?".

'Is there a problem?' Argon asked impatiently.

133

Evan met him with a level gaze but realised that he had no sway here.

'Satan would like to ask something,' he said firmly, but deep down knew that things were too far along to stop.

The room went quiet. Satan looked confused. A thought struck him he clicked his fingers and patted Evan on the arm, smiling.

'Do you know of any clay that might be around?'

'No, my Lord,' Argon said, as if he was well used to such strange and irrelevant outbursts from his strange and irrelevant leader.

Evan almost lost hope but then he had an idea.

'What Satan would like – and demands – is a detailed copy of plan "Homeland".'

Argon looked annoyed. 'Why?'

'He *is* your leader, isn't he? Your *Lord*. And as such he would like to be familiar with major decisions.'

'Very well,' he sneered, sliding sheaves of paper toward them.

Directly after work he went to the Human's Hovel and found the barman. He went down into the cellar and showed the barman the papers relating to operation "Homeland". The barman went white, and his hands shook as he read.

'This is it,' he said, 'This is the moment we've been waiting for.'

'Can I use your boat to intercept Purgatory as she sails past?' Evan asked, 'I have a friend onboard who can help me alert Heaven to the invasion.'

'Yes, of course, we have everything we need in those barrels.'

'The jellyfish?'

'We have most of the counterpart jellyfish of the oarsmen, that will be on Argon's war fleet. When the time comes, the brotherhood will terminate the jellyfish, thus robbing the fleet of its propulsion. That is our role.'

It was time for Evan to leave Hell. The barman told him that Purgatory was to sail past Hell sometime that night. He knew he must escape with Satan: as well as the documents, to help validate his story. He crept through the bowl, keeping to the parts that weren't lit by the few night-time torches. He climbed the walkway that led to the dark palace and went inside unnoticed. Satan was sitting in his mammal skull throne, next to the blazing fire, asleep. Evan shook his big red shoulder softly.

'Come on, time to go,' Evan said as he roused the dark prince.
'Where are we?' he answered sleepily.
'We're getting out - to a place where vegetables can grow.'

They left the Dark Palace and headed back down the long pathway that led to the base of the bowl. Evan had a large, purposeful stride, whereas Satan walked along as if on a woodland walk.

'Ooh! That's clay, isn't it?' Satan said excitedly pointing at the dusty red ground.
'We need to pick someone up on our way,' Evan said.

They reached Ivan's cage, and Evan nudged him through the bars.

'Hi Ivan. Do you remember me?' Evan asked.
Ivan looked at him, and then scowled.
'You! Evan Edwards! Damn you to Hell!' he said, then paused, and laughed.
'I'm here to get you out, come on,' Evan said opening the cage door with a master key Satan had provided.
Ivan rubbed his ceased knees, got up and joined them. They made their way to the beach and Evan found the recess in the

cliff where the Brotherhood's boat was tethered. Evan picked up a nearby jellyfish and began to pull at its tentacles and prod its nerve stem, before getting everyone in the boat and pushing off. They had just passed through Hell's dimensional membrane, when Ezekiel and his dolphin skidded up to the boat.

'Really, you must stop hurting my jellyfish,' he said to Evan.

'Sorry Ezekiel. I need you to find the counterpart jellyfish of anyone aboard Purgatory.'

Ezekiel gave him a suffering look, whipped his reigns and shot off into the blackness of the ether.

They floated in the ether, near to the dimensional membrane. Evan saw distant lights in the ether and knew it was Purgatory on its way back to Earth churning its way toward them. Ezekiel soon returned with the jellyfish. Evan gave Satan and Ivan an apologetic look before lying down in the boat and placing the jellyfish on his face.

Yuk

He looked around him and saw fake mahogany walls, with nautical paintings and thick red carpet under foot. It was Purgatory. He headed directly to the Mezzanine Bar. To his amazement Derek was using his mouth for something other than drinking and was in the middle of a lively conversation with a rubber plant. He pried his friend away and guided him out onto the Sun Deck for privacy. He shivered and turned to Evan.

'Get away from me, what do you want?' Derek shouted.

'No. Derek it's me, it's Evan, I'm just in a different body.'

'Evan my dear boy! What brings you back!' he said.

'Just focus a minute will you. I need you to do something for me. Something important, right now.'

'What's going on? I may be drunk, but I'm not stupid.

Evan quickly filled him in.

The Purgatory Plan

The rowboat closed in on Purgatory. The ether was calm. A crude rope dangled like an absurd draught excluder from the railings high above.

They climbed.

Evan was first over the railings, helped over by his friend.

'I've brought someone along,' Evan panted as he landed safely on deck.

Satan popped his head above the railings with his best attempt at an amiable smile.

'Arrggh!' Derek screamed as he desperately tried to undo the rope's knot and send the foul demon back into the ether.

'No wait. It's Satan!' Evan cried.

'What! Satan!' Derek screamed close to hysteria.

'Do you have any clay?' Satan asked placidly.

Derek passed out.

'I think he's coming around,' was the dream like sentence that Derek heard above his swimming head.

'Derek? Derek?' Evan said.

'Who is that?' Derek asked blearily, trying to get a handle on reality.

'I've already told you old man – this is Satan. And before you start screaming again, he's on our side.'

Derek realised that Evan had changed quite a bit since they were together on the ship. Like a puppy suddenly turning around and making you do the housework under its stern gaze.

'And you've got the bed sheets I told you to bring?' Evan asked.

'Right here.'

'Good,' Evan said, motioning for Satan to don the bedlinen in order to hide his red skin. He wanted to conceal Satan until the right moment came. The finished look was – unintentionally – that of a Muslim lady; with Satan being covered from head to toe, except for a small horizontal slit which he peaked out of.

Derek knew the ship better than any of them and so it was him that led the way to the Bridge. There was an open steel frame that led into the large room. There were four officers on duty (including the captain). The captain looked up from his cheese and cucumber sandwich, that he was meticulously constructing.

'Can I help?' he asked with undertones of *what the hell are you three doing on my bridge.*

'We need to talk with you,' Derek spoke up.

'Derek,' the captain began, well familiar with Purgatories longest standing oddity, 'I hope you are not about to cause trouble aboard my ship. If you wish to complain about the treatment given to you by the staff, then there are proper channels available to you...'

'You have to warn Heaven that they are in grave danger. A huge fleet of warships are sailing to its shores as we speak!'

The captain didn't need to be close to Derek to know that he was drunk. He had known that Derek was drunk and about to enter the bridge about six seconds before he walked in. It was the way that his cucumber slices wilted as he sliced them onto his sandwich.

'You're drunk,' The captain stated flatly, turning to his petty officers. 'Put all three of them in the Brig.'

'Run!' Derek said, and all four of them darted out of The Bridge. Evan reached into the pocket of his overalls and threw a penitence grenade into the middle of the room. The crew fell to their knees and stayed completely motionless in a prayer like position.

'What was that?' Derek demanded.

'Penitence grenade,' Evan replied smugly, 'Let's radio Heaven. Look, this is the frequency for the council building.'

The radio crackled and whirred until Evan found the correct frequency.

'Purgatory to council. Purgatory to council. Can you hear me over?'

'Yes Purgatory. This is the council over.'

'Listen carefully, I am here to warn you that Hell has sent a...

He couldn't say anymore because the line went dead.

Phillip Watts placed the bar-iron back into his tool bag. With Heaven's backup generator disabled, his plan was going to work, and Argon would be most pleased with him. The parts he had just destroyed were not replaceable (he had conveniently 'lost' the spares weeks ago). Heaven was now reliant on his turbines, and with the ether calm and flat...Fools.

Despondency fell upon the foursome.

'Bar anyone?' Derek suggested after a respectful silence.

'Not now. Of all the bloody times,' Evan rebuked scornfully. He then lapsed into deep thought. 'We just have to pray that the wind picks up,' he muttered quietly.

He looked up.

'Derek. Tell me again what drives the ether?'

'Inter-dimensional friction. Why?'

'Is it possible, that transferring minds from body to body, using inter-dimensional jellyfish, would create inter-dimensional friction?'

'It's possible.'

'Go to your cabin and get as many jellyfish as you have stored away, including one that connects to someone in Hell. I have a plan.'

The ship's announcement system crackled into life.

'Good afternoon, ladies and gentlemen,' Evan said, putting on his best captain's voice, 'The captain would like to invite all passengers to the Auditorium for a very special event. The purging supervisor is giving away absolution tokens, which passengers may use instead of attending purging sessions. The tokens are limited and will be distributed on a first come, first served basis. Thank you.'

Evan ran from the Bridge to the Auditorium balcony, whilst Derek, Satan and Ivan ran to his cabin to collect the jellyfish. The message had been more successful than he had anticipated and by the time he arrived, there were about thirty people milling around below him.

He pulled the pin and dropped the last penitence grenade. Everyone in the auditorium dropped to their knees, frozen nicely at prayer. He ran down a level, flew into the auditorium, shut all three access doors and wedged them shut with chairs. Evan then walked up to the nearest frozen passenger and pushed them onto their back, so that instead of kneeling on the ground facing forward; they had their knees sticking up into the air, praying skyward. Evan went around, doing the same to all of them.

Someone tried to open the main door. They tried again.

'Derek?' he hissed.

'Who is that? Open the door,' the unfamiliar voice demanded.

'Sorry can't,' Evan replied.

'Right, you'd better open this door right now or I'll report this to the captain.'

There was a dull thwack, followed by a heavy thud. 'It's me my boy,' Derek said through the door. Evan was never so glad to hear Derek's voice. He unhooked the chair and let him into the Auditorium. Satan and Ivan were close behind with bedsheets full of jellyfish.

They placed the jellyfish on to the passengers' faces until the tentacles slid into their ears.

Evan slumped down at one of the Auditorium's tables near the middle. The nervous energy he had been running on for the last hour had dissipated. Derek pulled up a chair and joined him – this could be the last time the two of would be together.

'Suppose it all goes to plan?' Evan started after a while.

'Yes?' Derek said.

'And the ether swells, and the wind blows, and Heaven is saved. What then?'

Derek sensed Evan's fatigue talking.

'Then it would be a miracle and a marvellous thing,' he replied encouragingly.

'Yes, but can people truly find happiness even if everything goes right?'

'How do you mean?'

'Well...I don't know...Heaven wasn't exactly my idea of utopia. Is there a place where someone can find real happiness?'

'Yes.'

'Where?'

'In there my boy.' Derek said as he leant across the table and tapped the side of Evan's head. 'In there.'

'Do you have that last jellyfish, the one to Hell?'

'Right here.'

Evan was in Hell again, in another unfamiliar body. He ran to the Human's Hovel and found the Brotherhood of Soul Releasers.

He persuaded them not to kill the counterpart jellyfish of the war fleet's oarsmen. Instead, they were to place the jellyfish on the faces of the Mind Soul Deteriorates. Evan explained about the possibility of friction being created; enough to perhaps create a breeze to turn Heaven's wind turbines. They agreed that an MSD would be incapable of rowing a ship and so promised to change their plans.

Evan woke back in the Auditorium and pulled the jellyfish off his face. Just as he was about tell Derek of his success, there was a huge grinding sound, and they were all thrown from their seats.

'What was that?!' Evan said, picking himself up from the floor.

'We've stopped,' Derek said, nursing a bruised arm.

'Sounded more like a crash,' Ivan said, limping over to them.

'What could we have crashed into?' Satan asked, completely fine.

'The only large object floating in the ether is Mount Purgatory, but why would the captain have crashed into the mountain?'

Everyone looked at one another and groaned, remembering that they had left the Bridge unmanned, except for four unconscious, praying crew.

Evan remembered what had been said on the tourist trip to the mountain all that time ago, that, the top of the mountain led to Eden, where one could talk directly to God Almighty. He grabbed Derek's beer-mat-rope, unhitched one of the chairs and left the auditorium, instructing the others to barricade it behind him and to hold out for as long as possible.

Scaling Mount Purgatory

Evan ran up to the Promenade Deck, past residents and crew members who were scurrying around, since the ship grounded. He tied one end of the rope to the railings and flung the other end down to the beach of the mountain. Once he had found footing on the sand, he raced up to the gate to the mountain and went through.

The first three terraces were deserted. The tourist attraction was not in operation. He crested the steps leading to the fourth level and ran along the terrace hoping to avoid the angel; no such luck. The soiled angel was sat on the steps leading up from the fourth terrace, spinning his rusty sword point down on the flint rock, causing tiny sparks to dance.

'I had a feeling that you would come back,' the angel said.

'I have to get to the top of this mountain, to get to Eden where I can talk directly to God!'

'I cannot let you up to the next level until you have been purged of the sin of slothfulness,' the angel explained.

Evan tried to barge past the angel, but he brought his sword up to Evan's throat. The angel, with some quick flicks of his wrist, cut four "P"s into Evan's forehead with the tip of his sword. Evan winced and recoiled in pain.

'What do I have to do?' Evan shuddered as blood began to trickle into his eye.

'First you must run up and down the length of this terrace ten times, just to give me time to think of something even more strenuous and befitting of your indolent life.'

Evan obeyed. The physical activity burnt away some of his fear and once finished he felt a little bolder.

'I want to explain something.'

'What is it?' the angel said impatiently. He was deep in thought coming up with horrendous activities for Evan to engage in.

'The thing is that I have changed between the time I died and now. It's true that I was lazy throughout my life, but since dying I've become much less slothful.'

'I don't care. Do you know how long it's been since I have been able to purge someone?'

'Five centuries?'

'Yes, my life's work is on this terrace, the pride of my profession. I can't let you through until you are purged.'

'How long will it take?'

The angel sucked air through his lips.

'Not long really. Not in the great scheme of things. Ten years, give or take a year. Now if you've finished speaking, you can get back to running whilst I get out the boulder and chain.'

The angel got out his boulder and checked that the chain attachment was still in working order. It was a little rusty, but serviceable. He called out to the running Evan to stop and join him so that he could chain him to it. He let the angel put the chains around his shoulders. Once strapped in, he made it look like he was trying to pull the boulder, whilst making painful groaning noises.

'I can't seem to get it to move,' Evan said.

'Pah, weakling,' the angel snorted.

'Maybe if you showed me how, I might be able to do it,' Evan suggested.

The angel stroked his matted beard, 'I suppose that there is a knack to it.'

The angel detached Evan from the boulder before attaching himself.

'The trick is to make sure the shoulder straps are good and tight, so that there's no way of freeing yourself.'

'That looks like it could be a little tighter,' Evan said as he tightened down the angel's shoulder straps even more.

'Steady, you're cutting off the circulation,' The angel protested.

Evan smiled as he walked around to boulder and started to push it off the terrace's cliff face.

'What are you doing!' The angel shrieked when he realised what was happening.

'Sorry, but I can't wait ten years, I hope you come through this in one piece.'

The boulder teetered on the edge of the terrace and then plummeted down, with the angel in tow. He spread his malting wings like a parachute and landed awkwardly on the terrace below. Evan dashed up the steps and onto the fifth terrace.

The fifth terrace was silent except for the quiet sound of metal objects clinking against each other. Sitting on the next set of steps was another angel, playing with shiny objects within a small chest. On seeing Evan, he smacked shut the lid and placed it behind himself.

'What are you doing on my terrace?' The angel asked with annoyance in his voice.

'I'm going to the top of the mountain,' Evan replied.

'Why you, why now?

'Which sin did you purge on this level?'

'Avaricious people are purged on my terrace.'

'Surely you could just let me past, after all, who would know?'

The angel thought and then noticed Evan's digital watch. 'What is that on your wrist?' he asked pointing.

'It's a watch, it tells the time,' Evan said realising that the angel had never seen a wrist watch before.

'That's amazing! Give it to me.'

'Will you let me past if I do?'

'Maybe.'

Evan undid his watch and handed it to the angel. The angel inspected it carefully, his eyes becoming brighter and more excited. He pulled out his chest from its hiding place, opened it and carefully placed the watch within. Evan was able to briefly see into the chest, which was full of gold coins, rings and silver jewellery.

'What does avaricious mean?'

'The love of wealth and material things,' the angel said as he clicked shut the lid of his chest and slid it behind himself.

'Can I go through now then?'

'No. I think that you are still far too attached to material things. This is an awful sin and I must help you to overcome it. The only way to purge you fully is for you to remove all of your material clothing.'

'What!'

'You heard me, get naked, like Adam and Eve before they knew of sin.'

Evan didn't have the time to argue with him and so he removed all of his clothes and gave them to the angel. The naked Evan coughed to get the angel's attention.

'Very well, through you go.' The angel healed one of the P's from Evan's forehead as he went past.

Cresting onto the sixth terrace, he saw a large apple tree sprouting from the rock. Its branches held sweet, ripe apples and was shaped like an inverted fir tree, getting broader as it went up. A stream fell from the mountain above, onto the tree, drenching all of its leaves. Out of curiosity, Evan reached up to take one of the lower hanging apples.

'I wouldn't do that if I were you,' the sixth terrace angel warned as she came into sight from further around the curve of the mountain. 'Those apples never satiate your appetite. They are designed to make you even hungrier as a punishment for your greed. Welcome to the terrace of the gluttonous. Feel free to progress to the next level, I will not stop you.'

Evan looked confused. 'Why?' he asked dubiously.

'To tell the truth, I don't want to be here. I'd rather be in Heaven soaking up the glory of God and mingling with the Heavenly Host. Except that I can't because to get off this blasted mountain, I have to get down past the fourth terrace.' The angel actually flinched as he mentioned the place. 'And you know who guards that.'

'Yes I met the angel, he seems to take a lot of pride in his work.'

'He's *insane,*' the angel spat, 'keeping the three of us on this redundant mountain to protect it from demons. Demons! They never venture further than their torture pits. They have no interest in Mount Purgatory.'

'Well, between you and me, your colleague that guards the fourth terrace is currently guarding the third terrace with a heavy boulder chained to him, so if you're quick...'

'Much obliged,' called the angel as she healed another P from Evan's forehead and flew down the stairs.

The seventh level of Mt Purgatory consisted of a field of tall, clear flames, held back from a narrow path along the edge of the terrace by a strong wind rising from below. The angel guarding the terrace of lust wandered aimlessly between the flames.

'Hello,' the angel greeted him. 'Stand in one of the flames and be purged of your excessive lust in life.'

'Will it take long?'

'No, but it is very painful.'

'Good enough for me,' he said as he stepped boldly into the nearest flame. The pain was instant. He tried to scream but nothing came out. His flesh seared and his blood boiled. Images and feelings of lust ran rampant through his mind, completely out of his control. Before he knew it he had passed out and awoke on the floor of the seventh terrace with no pain in his body.

'You have been purged of lust my boy,' said the angel sympathetically, 'and the fires that I tend, thank you for giving them the first taste of human flesh in over five hundred years.' The angel helped Evan to his feet and healed a third P from his forehead, leaving one P remaining.

'Go now to Eden,' the angel said, pointing to the final set of steps leading up to the top of the mountain, where a porthole of searing white light stood. Evan scrambled up the last few meters and went straight through.

Second Coming Ward

The naked Evan emerged, drenched in sweat, into dense tropical vegetation. He sank to his knees in the mossy undergrowth, breathing quickly, gasping for the precious oxygen that his quavering muscles demanded. A multitude of palms, exotic and broad leafed species surrounded him at close quarters and in all directions. The deep throbbing of blood in his ears had subsided and he now heard the sound of babbling conversation.

Although thickly planted, the vegetation let through streams of light and as he looked at these dust speckled shafts, Evan noticed that they came and went like the turning on and off of a light switch. The small gaps in the foliage would momentarily change colour as if different objects were coming and going on the other side. Evan was confused and decided that it was time to talk directly with the God. He cleared his mind, breathed deeply and raised his palms to the air. 'O Lord, can you hear me?'

The response came within seconds. A crackled, nasal voice answered him: 'A notice for the public. The Eden Project cafeteria has a special on all breakfast muffins, so grab a bite before exploring nature's wonders.'

Evan, on his knees, arms stretched to the Heavens, let out a cry of despair. He dropped his arms and grasped at the soil, pulling up moss and any other vegetation that was within reach. His exhausted body quivered and he fought back the sobs that wanted to rob him of his momentum. With great sweeps of his arms, he tore back the vegetation, wild eyed, and stumbled out onto a gravelled walkway.

'You!' He said gruffly to a frightened child that he had wrenched from the peripheries of a school group. The little girl's eyes were wide with shock. 'Where am I?' the naked Evan demanded of the eight-year-old. 'Is this paradise? How do I get to someone who knows about Purgatory?!!'

By the time her teacher had rushed over, the little girl's eyes were watering and her bottom lip was quivering.

'What are you doing!' The teacher screeched.

'Maybe you know,' Evan said turning to the teacher. The assistant to the teacher looked over from where she was a few metres away, and began to wade through the sea of school children to see what was happening.

'Know what?' The teacher said placing her arms on her hips, 'Know why a naked lunatic with a P cut into his forehead is grabbing and scaring a little girl?'

'Sorry, she was just the nearest person.'

By now the assistant had reached them. 'What's the matter Sue?' the assistant asked concerned.

'Go and alert the authorities that there is a strange naked man scaring children, and *touching* them.' She added accusingly, narrowing her eyes.

'WHAT?!' Evan said. 'What do you mean by that!' The assistant hesitated, but one iron look from teacher Sue sent her scurrying off to the nearest information desk.

'We're in a public place and you could see us!' he objected.

'It's still wrong.' She snorted resolutely. Evan shook his head in disbelief. The little girl looked up and him and giggled. The security guards were not as enamoured with Evan's appearance. They grabbed him, twisted his arm behind his back and forced him face down onto the floor.

'Bloody nonce!' one of the guards grunted.

Evan tried to respond, but his mouth was full of gravel.

Evan was placed in a prison cell and the door was slammed home. He slumped onto the blue, laminate mattress and felt hopeless. The invasion fleet was on its way to Heaven, and he was here, somehow back on Earth, unable to warn them.

Two hours passed before the door was re-opened. A tall middle aged woman with a serious expression and blue cardigan came in. She approached Evan with a cautious smile.

'Hello,' the psychiatrist said as she crouched down so as to be on the same level as Evan. He looked into her friendly, searching eyes and felt his best choice was to explain the whole situation and hope that she was able to put him in touch with someone who could help.

He explained of his dying and going aboard Purgatory, of Heaven and Jennifer, Hell and ending up beached on the shores of Mt Purgatory. She took all of this information in with professional ease, with smatterings of encouraging nods and murmurs. Once he had finished, she drew herself up and left the cell. The door was once again shut and locked. Evan noticed that the door was not slammed this time, but rather pressed into place.

Another hour passed. The door was re-opened by two of the policemen.

'Come on lad, time to go,' one of them said.

'Go where?'

'We're taking you to hospital, come along now.'

'I don't want to go. I'm not ill. I thought you were going to help me.'

'We are going to help you, and with the right medication, you'll put all these strange thoughts behind you and get on with your life.'

Evan let out another cry of despondency.

The policemen escorted Evan down the long colourful corridors strewn with potted plants and artwork. A man with long brown hair, wispy beard and white dressing gown, drifted past them with a serene look on his face. After a few turns and wide double doors, they came to a sturdy single door with a red switch embedded on the wall next to it. Above the thick door was a blue plaque that read "Second Coming Ward" in large lettering. The policeman pressed the switch and a nurse on the other side opened the door, using a key that jingled by his thigh. They went in and followed the male nurse - who wore a bright red tank top and brown loafers - to the admissions room. The medication room opposite was open for business. Two nurses bustled within, cracking open strips of medication, filling small plastic containers with water and chatting with the patients. The queue was long and lined the corridor.

'Thank you, officer,' he said to the policeman, 'we can manage from now'. The policemen nodded and went back to the ward exit where another nurse let them out.

'My name is Carl. Would you like something to eat? It was fish cakes for lunch and there should be some left.'

Evan nodded morosely.

Carl reappeared ten minutes later with a plate of fish cake bits in a little mound.

'Sorry about this: Robert was trying to feed the five thousand again. This is all I could salvage,' he said with an apologetic smile.

By the time he was led out of the admissions room, the corridor was quiet. Carl pointed toward the common room door as he went back to the central nurse's station to pick up a ringing telephone. Evan pushed open the common room door and went inside. The room was large and filled with two sofas, hard backed chairs, tables and a pool table. It was full of men and women reading, playing pool or just sitting looking around. The man in the white dressing gown and wispy beard he had passed in the corridor was now sat on one of the sofas. Next to him was another man, different in build and facial structure, but with biblical robes and a much darker, fuller beard; which Evan recognised as Jesus: the man he had seen in the caravan in Heaven. The wispy bearded man spread his palms upon the low coffee table between the two sofas, with the loaf of bread between his hands. Drawing breath he picked it up and tore it in half. He took each half and in turn tore it into quarters. The patients sitting around him looked on with interest apart from Jesus who looked bored with his neighbours exploits.

'You've already tried that with the fish cake Robert,' Jesus said to the man breaking the bread, 'and it didn't work.'

'Silence impostor,' Robert snapped. 'Everyone knows that I'm the real Jesus, not you.'

'You're not Jesus, I am,' Jesus said in exasperation.

'No you're not,' Robert protested. 'You're just some nut who thinks that he's Jesus! Why do you think they put you in here?!'

'I know, it's starting to annoy me,' Jesus said. 'This is my seventh attempt at coming back to Earth. But as soon as I open my mouth to anyone and explain who I am, they can't get to a phone quick enough to call an ambulance.'

'If you are the real Jesus then tell us a parable,' Robert challenged. The other patients sat in the common room all nodded in agreement with this suggestion. Evan, who had been standing in the doorway came and sat down in one of the hard backed chairs next to the real Jesus.

Jesus cleared his throat and the common room hushed. It would have been silence if it wasn't for the group of men playing pool and chatting loudly, seemingly unaware of the poignant messages about to be divulged. After a moment to gather his thoughts he began.

'There was a man who smoked forty cigarettes a day. He wanted to quit and so put it to his doctor, that if he ran out of both tobacco and papers, he would not buy any more. Many weeks of heavy smoking passed, until the day he ran out of both. Then he put it to his doctor, that if he ran out of tobacco, papers *and* filters he would quit. He continued heavily smoking for some months, until the day he ran out of all three. He looked upon the lighter in his hand and put it to his doctor, that if he were to run out of tobacco, papers, filters *and* lighter fluid at the same time, he would quit smoking. He died a painful death soon after.'

Jesus, formally known as Robert, tugged at his wispy beard in annoyance.

'Such a clever tongue you have impostor of Nazareth,' Robert chided. 'Take your oily tongue away to your bedroom anti-Christ!'

They all looked at him in surprise.

Jesus sighed and got up to leave. Evan grabbed his arm and pulled him back into his chair.

'I think we should hear Robert tell us a parable, if he is the real Jesus that is.'

Robert shifted in his chair, rearranged his dressing gown and straightened to full height. His face went blank for a moment as he gathered his thoughts.

'I will now recant the parable of the transgender toilet attendant.' He cleared his throat before continuing to speak to the variably dressed patients.

'Once there was a transgender individual who gained employment as a toilet attendant in a busy night club. She was born a man, but decided to become a woman. As far as the night club management could tell, he was a woman.'

'What about her Adam's apple?' one of the patients asked.

'She had it surgically removed,' Robert replied.

'What about her unusually large hands and feet?' another patient persisted.

'She had them surgically removed as well,' he replied shortly.

'You mean she didn't have any hands or feet? How did she do her job then?' the first patient asked.

'She had hooks,' Robert replied without thinking. He paused and frowned. 'No wait that isn't going to work. Let's just say that she was a very delicately framed man to begin with and already had small womanly hands and feet.'

'I was quite interested in how the hooks were going to pan out but hey,' the first patient said, genuinely disappointed.

'There isn't much broad appeal to this parable is there, I mean it's about a transsexual with hooks for limbs,' the second patient critiqued.

'Shut up!' Robert snapped, throwing a gardening magazine at the heckler, 'I haven't finished yet and I've already scrapped the hooks. As I was saying. The management didn't know and so placed her in the women's toilet to hand out perfume and sexual advice or whatever female toilet attendants do.'

'This is rubbish,' the first patient stated bluntly.

'Shut up!' He screeched, upping the ballistic retaliation to a hard backed book. 'She had, however, forgotten to take her hormone repression tablets and her natural testosterone levels were sky high, causing her to be extremely attracted to the women who came in and out of the toilet.'

'Does anyone want a coffee?' the first heckler asked nursing his arm where the corner of the book had struck him. Four of the group nodded amiably and the next minute was taken up by differing requests for milk and sugar. Once the heckler was in the kitchen, he continued.

'One day the urges were too strong and she was caught spying into a toilet cubicle by the management.'

'Is that it? What's the moral to that?' the second patient said with a frown and a laugh.

'Don't forget to take your hormone repression tablets,' the first patient called out loudly from the kitchen as the kettle boiled. Many laughed, but some were too ill to understand and just looked back and forth at those speaking.

'No. It's about the inevitability of God's creation winning over manipulation by man,' Robert said flapping his arms in desperation. 'How we try to change ourselves through man made mediums such as surgery and hormone tablets, but the nature that God gave us is unsurpassed, such as being born a man.'

A patient who had been silent roused himself from inner thoughts to speak, 'It's not in keeping with current social thinking. It sounds like environmental determinism as opposed to the contemporary move toward personal potentiality.'

Robert gasped and fled to his bedroom, his white dressing gown flapping behind him.

Evan beckoned Jesus to follow him to an empty part of a corridor.

'What are you doing here?' Evan asked. 'The last time I saw you, you were in your caravan in Heaven.'

Jesus looked surprised at the mention of his caravan.

'You're the gardener who was outside weeding my vegetable plot. What are you doing here?'

'I need to get back to Heaven to warn them, an invasion fleet from Hell, led by Argon, is sailing to Heaven as we speak.'

'That's quite a tall tale...'

'Look, you recognise me from Heaven, so you know I'm not just a mad person like the rest of them in here. I did have a detailed copy of their plans, but it was taken from me when I was scaling Mt Purgatory. Either way, I need your support when I get to the council of Heaven, if I ever get back to Heaven. You just have to trust me.'

'Fine, this holiday has taken a turn for the worse anyway.'

'So how do we get back to Heaven?'

'Suicide,' Jesus said.

'What?!' Evan gasped.

'We die and end up in the company of St Peter; I explain the situation and he lets us into Heaven.'

'How do we...do that then.'

'Follow me. There is a place in the garden, a wooden fence that is completely hidden from the nurses station and the rest of the ward.'

They made their way into the garden, found the blind spot that Jesus was talking about and heaved themselves over the wooden fence. They scampered down the grass bank on the other side of the fence and ran onto the main road that ran past the psychiatric hospital. Cars sped toward them.

Zoom zoom zoom.

Zoom - **Splat.**

Zoom - **Splat.**

Heaven Prepares for Battle

The council of Heaven was dubious about Evan's testimony, but backed up by Jesus, they begrudgingly agreed to send out a reconnaissance angel to investigate. Their light hearted jesting stopped abruptly when the news came back that there were over a hundred ships on course to Heaven's harbour.

'The back up generator!' One of the council members, Solomon, exclaimed, 'The back up generator is down, we need to get it fixed at once. If the wind doesn't blow, its all we have to power our defences. We need to contact God.'

'He switches off his mobile when on holiday. This is why we started the wind power programme, remember?' Mr Watts said. The other council members murmured in agreement.

'Yes but it's completely untested!' Solomon retorted.

'I trust Mr Watts completely,' Magnus, the council leader, said. 'If he says he can fix the generator, than he can fix it.'

'Perhaps the maintenance manager could help you?' Evan said, remembering Tom's workshop.

'No,' Mr Watts said quickly 'It is highly technical work, I couldn't risk a pair of unskilled hands.'

'But we need to arm ourselves!' Solomon insisted, 'We need to be ready if the defences have no power!'

'We only have ceremonial weaponry, since the defections.' A member said.

Magnus called the meeting to a close.

Evan and Jesus were walking away from the council building when Solomon came bounding up to them.

'Something is wrong. We need to do something.' He said flatly, close to Jesus' ear.

Jesus smiled and led the way to the woodland behind his caravan. He stopped them when they reached a clearing.

'Come on, help me move this bracken,' Jesus said. They revealed wooden double doors leading down into the ground. Jesus unlocked the chain holding it together and then flung open both doors. A billow of dust blew up out of the opening and they all turned their eyes away and spluttered.

'Sorry; I haven't been in here for a while,' he said.

He went down and pulled on a cord which triggered a bright, bare bulb.

Their eyes bulged as they looked inside.

'Just a little collection of mine,' Jesus said, standing in his bunker stacked with various weaponry. 'Come in, come in,' he beckoned. Small arms made up the majority of the collection. They were stacked neatly on racks on the left hand wall – from floor to ceiling – and included mainly AK47s but also other rifles such as American M16s, and British SA80s. Three heavy machine guns – two GPMGs and a Bren Gun were on the floor at the rear, set up on bi-pods. Rocket propelled grenade launchers and a single laser guided rocket launcher – of which Jesus was particularly proud – were in racks at the back. The other side of the bunker held the ammunition.

'How?' Evan asked confused. 'How can you get away with having all this stuff?'

Jesus smiled, 'Well dad knows about it of course, but then again I did suffer horrific torture and die on the cross at Calvary for him, so he turns a blind eye to it.'

'So how did Solomon know?'

'I helped him smuggle all of this in,' Solomon said. 'I never did agree with the disarmament treaty signed by the council.'

'If we've got as little time as you say, we'd better get moving,' Jesus said. 'Solomon, grab that mega phone and I'll get the quad bike.'

The grandmaster of the Soul Releaser Society was getting anxious. The time for action was approaching, and even though a peaceful man, he knew what had to be done for the greater good. He only required minimal communication with his fellow brothers to get the scene going. All members of the Brotherhood were now well familiar with the revised plan to save Heaven. The grandmaster walked a lap of the great bowl, making eye contact with his single, scarred eye, to those that he needed. They stopped what they were doing and fell into step behind him. On the second lap, and with about twenty brothers with him, he got out his master key and began to open the cages of the damned. He chose the cages carefully, opening the ones which were in the later stages of the Ongoing Productive Torture. People who had endured decades of brutal torture at the hands of the demons, but who were not so far gone into Mind Soul Deterioration to not be of any use. The damned looked confused, not understanding why the cages were being opened.

'Come my brothers,' the grandmaster said, 'step out of your cages and join us.'

One of the damned worked up the moisture to speak, 'what will happen to us?'

'You will be free to do as you wish.'

'Can we kick the crap out of the demons?'

The grandmaster smiled, 'With my blessing, you can.'

Jesus and Solomon first went down to the beach. It was a glorious morning and many people were there, sunning themselves or doing activities. Jesus was going full throttle churning up the sand with his wide tires. Solomon was mounted on the back, holding on with the mega phone flailing wildly by his side. They slowed as they reached the first group of residents.

'PEOPLE OF HEAVEN. YOU ARE ALL IN GRAVE DANGER. HELL IS INVADING. I REPEAT, HELL IS INVADING. THEY WILL BE ON

OUR SHORES IN A MATTER OF HOURS. PLEASE REPORT TO THE SUN PLAZA IMMEDIATELY FOR ARMAMENT AND BASIC TRAINING. THANK YOU.'

Within fifteen minutes, the beach was empty and the residents had grabbed their belongings and hurriedly made their way up the hill to the plaza. The angels that had been taking the various activity classes came up to Solomon and asked him angrily about what was going on. After he had explained the situation and told them their plan, they agreed to rally the other angels and help keep order with the growing crowd of residents in the Sun Plaza.

The Sun Plaza was packed by the time Jennifer, Susan and Tom arrived. The angels were already dressed in their highly polished armour and had full control of the jittery crowd. Jennifer saw Evan and came bounding up to him.

'I'm so glad to see you!' she said in a scared voice. 'What's going on? People are talking about an invasion!'

'Yes it's true, but don't worry, I'm sure the defences will work,' Evan said to reassure her.

Tom went up to the archangel Francis and had a quiet chat with him, both their faces deadly serious as they talked. Francis nodded, grabbed the soap box and mounted it. Everyone who saw this went quiet and soon the hush spread to the rest of the crowd.

'People of Heaven,' he began, 'as you have already heard, we will very soon be under attack.' The crowd broke down into various noises. Francis raised his hand to silence them. 'However we are only gathered here as a precaution: it is unlikely that any of you will have to fight. Not as long as the normal defences hold, but we believed that it would be better to prepare you just in case...'

'WHAT IS THIS!' The leader of the council boomed as he strode into the plaza with Phillip Watts skulking behind him. 'Francis! Get down from there at once. And the rest of you – go back to your normal activities!'

'We thought that...' Francis started.

'You thought nothing!' Magnus chastised. 'It is the job of the council to think and make decisions, not the angels! The council has made its decision...'

'To do nothing,' Francis said coldly.

'...to put its faith in the defences! Do you remember what faith is Francis?'

'Don't you dare lecture me on faith you dry old man,' he said with venom. 'You may be the president of the council, but I have been here since the creation and led the expulsion of the dark angels during the great defection. That was a test of faith greater than sitting around pinning all of our hopes on those white spinning toilet brushes!'

There was a cheer from the crowd who had been listing carefully to the bout of their leadership. It was now clear to the president who the people were going to follow. He and Mr Watts left the plaza defeated.

Francis continued and asked for anyone with military experience to come forward. The number that volunteered was disappointingly small. There was Tom; a Lance Corporal by the name of Atkins, who had died in the Great War; an English knight from the first crusade by the name of Medley who had jumped into his steel armour on the first mention of a battle; and Lylo, a Vietnamese soldier.

The angels divided the more able looking residents into groups of about twenty people each. Francis organised his angels and told them to distribute the arms. The first group were fitted out with the AK47's; a second group were given a mixture of the M16's and SA80's; whereas the stronger looking residents had been separated and were handed the RPG launchers. Finally the ammunition and grenades were distributed. The residents looked uneasy handling the objects in their hands. They inspected the rifles clumsily and then looked at each other with worried expressions.

Francis got back on his box. 'You will now be instructed on how to use the weapons that you have been given.'

He signalled to Tom, Lylo and Jesus who were stood at the side. The three of them took a group each and sat them down in loose circles in different corners of the plaza.

They began to teach.

'This is the AK47,' Lylo said to his group, lifting the Kalashnikov out in front of him. 'It is the most ubiquitous rifle in the world and is the most simple to use. It works by a simple gas operated bolt-firing system and has only eight moving parts. Yet is capable of releasing 650 rounds per minute...'

'This is the SA80,' Tom started with his group. 'Considering the time scale, we will concentrate on loading, unloading, stoppages and sight settings...'

By the time half an hour had passed, Lylo's group were happily stripping, assembling, loading, cocking and unloading their simple Kalashnikovs. Tom had taught the loading and unloading but still had to teach them to deal with stoppages. Not to mention get on and teach the American rifles. After another half an hour had passed, Tom knew that time was getting short. He got up and briefly left his group to speak with Francis.

'This is taking longer than I expected,' Tom said flatly.

'All of the angels are ready for battle,' Francis replied.

'You should take your angels and those who are ready and start organising the defences of the harbour.'

'Very well, what will you do?'

'Teach. And pray. Oh yes and be sure to save three choice spots for the machine guns, I've got just the boys for the job.'

He went back to his group after a brief word with Atkins, Medley and Lylo, and carried on with his lesson. Soon the plaza began to empty of people as the residents trudged out to the shore under the leadership of Francis.

Once the remaining residents had received a rudimentary lesson on the M16 they were told to join the others on the dock. Only Atkins, Medley and Lylo remained.

'Right then,' Tom said gleefully rubbing his hands together and then pointing to the heavy machine guns set up on the floor, 'my main men.'

'What is that?' Medley said with disdain as he pointed to the Machine gun.

'That is a Bren Gun my dear Medley.'

'Well I'm quite happy with my broad sword thank you very much,' The knight sniffed.

'Look Medley.' Tom said shortly. 'I need disciplined men on these things – military men. In the wrong hands, they could do more damage than good.'

'Well, that one looks more effective than those two ugly things,' he said pointing to the Bren Gun.

'It's yours.' He turned back to talk to the others.

'Can I name it?' Medley continued.

'What?'

'Name it. Like I name my sword, for luck.'

'Yes, knock yourself out.'

'Thank you.'

'Right then' Tom continued. 'Get into the prone position and I'll run through how to use them.'

Once finished they jogged out to the dock. Tom told Lylo to stay near to the entrance of the Sun Plaza. He then instructed Medley and Atkins to take up their positions – one either side of the harbour entrance. They were as ready as they'd ever be.

The riot in Hell was in full progress. The Brotherhood had unleashed over a hundred of the damned, who now stalked around in large hungry packs, hunting down the demon oppressors with zeal. Being unarmed, many were wounded by tridents, but their overwhelming numbers made up for any set backs. Soon they acquired weapons from those they had swamped, and moved on with even more confidence. The Brotherhood now had their chance to do their part. They gathered in the cellar of the Human's Hovel and quickly set about finding the counterpart jellyfish of those who were now rowing the invasion fleet across the ether. Placing the jellyfish into a beer barrel, they heaved it up the stairs and out into the street. The demons were too busy trying to put down the riot to notice the half dozen humans rolling a beer barrel across the bowl and toward the Mind Soul Deteriorates.

Evan, Jennifer and Susan were posted on the left-hand arm of the seawall, about half a mile out from the shore. They lay down on their stomachs as they had been taught and poked the muzzles of their rifles through the parapet.

'I can't stand not knowing what's going on.' Evan said irritably. Jennifer pointed up at the angels who were populating the sky above.

'I think they're sending out patrols to track the progression of the fleet.' She checked that her magazine was in properly but wasn't sure so she pulled it out and rammed it back until it gave a healthy *click*.

Susan was sobbing quietly. Jennifer rubbed her back in an attempt to comfort her.

Then the light breeze that was blowing stopped. The minority of the turbines that had been slowly swishing around now stood perfectly still.

'Oh no,' Evan said.

'What? What's wrong?' Jennifer asked.

'The wind has stopped. The turbines aren't producing any power.'

The attack fleet was approaching the dimensional membrane of Heaven, when a white carpet of jellyfish glided in from below and stopped in front of it, blockading the way. Ezekiel, the jellyfish herder, hovered on his dolphin steed at the head of his jellyfish army. Drawing his sword, he rubbed his dolphin's head, who had insisted on being painted up with lightning bolts down his side; a kamikaze bandanna wrapped about his dorsal fin; and "kiss my blow hole" written on his smooth head. Ezekiel rode to the back of the shoal and began to herd the jellyfish toward the fleet.

Argon did not know what was happening, or what was coming toward him before it was too late. The shoal engulfed the ships, attaching themselves to the faces of the demons and dark angels. The fleet began to go awry, as they were transported, at random into different bodies and different dimensions, causing some ships to break formation and drift off to the side. Ezekiel charged his steed forward to the nearest ship and began to cut down the incapacitated demons where they stood.

The dark angels and demons quickly pulled the jellyfish free from their fellows and steered the fleet back into formation. Ezekiel was busily taking on an entire ship single handed, his white sword thrashing against the enemy. The jellyfish had long since given up their pitiful offensive and had decided to regroup somewhere off to the side and amuse themselves by making geometrical shapes in the ether. Ezekiel, now completely alone and surrounded by demons and their bristling weapons, took a moment to pause and assess his situation. He looked over to his jellyfish army, which was just putting the finishing touches to a dodecahedron. His dolphin sensed the danger and took him away from the ships and toward the dimensional membrane of Heaven.

Word quickly spread that the generator was out of action. Panic gripped the residents. The fact that the residents were strung out so thinly along the seawall, meant that the panic they experienced was personalised and isolated. When Jennifer turned back to look at the sea, her heart sank lower than it had ever sunk before as she saw the fleet for the first time. She then heard one of the machine guns mounted on the harbour entrance open up. A few seconds later the other one opened. She tightened her grip on the rifle with one hand and reached out for Evan's hand with the other.

The first few machine gun shots took Argon by surprise. A bullet glanced off his shoulder armour, leaving behind a nasty scratch on the gold plating. He realised that Heaven still had some fight left in them and so he would retire to the safety of the rear of the fleet until the invasion was over. He was about to give the order for his leading vessel to break away from the formation when he heard a faint whistling sound.

The force of the rocket propulsion knocked Jesus clean off his feet, sending him clattering to the ground in a heap of sandals, robes, long hair, and state-of-the-art electronically guided rocketry. There was a colossal explosion which ripped through the calm blue day. The leading vessel de-atomised under the force of Jesus' rocket. When the smoke cleared, Argon was no more.

The battle, however, was far from over. Other dark angels were waiting in the wings to take over and they kept the fleet together and moving toward the harbour entrance. There was, however, a problem with the oarsmen. The demons on the ships went below decks to see what the problem was. Most of their oarsmen were just sitting there with vacant expressions, dribbling. No matter how much the demons whipped them, they would not row.

Jesus' RPG battalion knelt, strung out either side of the machine gun posts. As the fleet began to drift into the harbour entrance, the RPG's started to fire as the inexperienced residents got the feel of their weapons. The first few volleys were completely ineffectual – either falling too short or too long. Jesus shouted at them to adjust their sight settings as the vessels drifted nearer.

Only a few accurate grenades were fired before the dark angels and demons on deck were close enough to discharge their concentrated flame bursts. The residents were forced to take cover behind the parapet.

Medley and Atkinson fared better. Nicely snuggled into the parapet, their machine guns cut the decks of the ships to pieces as they sailed past the entrance – forcing the demons to dive for cover. Medley stopped firing and looked over to Jesus who was crouched behind the parapet with his battalion. Medley raised his gauntleted hand and made a "turn around" signal. Jesus looked behind him toward the dock and realised what he meant. The ships which had made it through the entrance were in shabby order after being ripped though by the GPMG and Bren Gun.

Jesus shouted out to his group to turn and fire on the vulnerable vessels. They didn't seem to understand or more likely - didn't want to, because it meant emerging from the safety of cover. Jesus loaded his RPG, picked out a vessel, stood up quickly and made a snap shot before diving back down to cover, as a flame burst just missed his head. A couple of the more confident residents followed his lead and took out another two vessels. Before long they were all at it. Jumping up; firing; diving back down; moving a bit; and jumping up again.

The dynamic between the machine guns and rocket launchers was working well - until they ran out of ammunition. Jesus knew that they could do no more good and so hurried his residents back down the seawall to relative safety.

The angels, in the meantime, were in the skies above the fleet trying to do what damage they could. The innate power within them meant that they could fire pure white light from their swords, neutralising the demons. They were, however, grossly out numbered and taking heavy flak from the flame bursts being shot into the air at them from the sword tips of the massed dark angels. Francis ordered them to fall back behind the seawall.

The tentative advantage soon tipped as the sheer number of Hell's minions overwhelmed the small band of Heaven's fighting force. The order was given to move back to the dock. The angels did their best to cover the retreat of the frightened residents as they ran all the way back along the seawall. Medley and Atkinson had long since run out of ammunition and had left their red hot machine guns where they lay.

The residents and angels made a new and more concentrated defensive line on the dock. They found positions and cover as best they could. Lylo was up on the roof of the building that separated the Sun Plaza from the dock. Tom was lying next to him acting as a spotter for last the machine gunner.
They noticed that the fleet had stopped moving. They did not know why. It bought them some time, but time for what? There was nothing to stop the minions of Hell now, no matter how slowly they advanced.

Many of the others decided to climb up on the various buildings which lined the dock – it seemed to be the safest place to fight from. The angels hovered above. This was their last stand. Beyond this there was only broken and desperate fighting in and around the villas.

Each and every resident and angel tried to convince themselves that they had a chance. In their heart of hearts, they knew they were done for. The initial skirmish in the harbour had only dealt with about twenty or thirty vessels. The vast majority of the fleet was now making its menacingly slow journey to the dock.

A despondent silence enveloped the residents as they awaited their doom. Then Jennifer stood up and pointed out to sea.

'Look!' she shouted in a tone completely at odds with the general mood.

A strong off-shore wind began to blow.

The turbines creaked and moaned.

They held their breath and clasped one another.

The turbines turned.

The front of the fleet was halfway across the expanse of the harbour when the two giant stone angels came sleepily to life. They opened their great eyes and flexed their stiff, ancient, stone muscles. The left hand angel looked casually behind him and saw the fleet creeping its way to the dock. He rolled his eyes and tapped his right hand colleague on the shoulder. They simultaneously turned around and bathed the whole of Heaven in a blinding whiteness from the tips of their huge swords.

Utopia

'Are you happy?' Jennifer asked dreamily.

'At this very moment I'm happy,' he answered.

'Good,' she smiled.

She got out of bed, switched off the light and returned to Evan's arms...

Susan waved Derek off as he boarded Purgatory for another planned relapse. St Peter had allowed him into Heaven due to his part in saving Paradise. Purgatory, however, was still the only place in the afterlife to get a decent drink, and Derek could not bring himself to dry off completely. He needed it less since he met Susan, but old dogs don't change overnight...

The Tuesday morning pottery class had a new and enthusiastic member. By the end of the month he was running the class. Jesus decided to make a large joint vegetable garden with him, and in years to come new generations of residents would tell of hearing laughter from the inseparable gardeners.

Printed in Great Britain
by Amazon